THE GHOST ROCK CAFE

THE GHOST ROCK CAFE

CHINLE MILLER

Yellow Cat
PUBLISHING

Cover by Cary Cox.

For Roger

CONTENTS

1

Bud Shumway pushed his dark brown sunglasses up onto the bridge of his nose, where, like fresh tar running down a sloped roof, they slowly began their journey back down to the end of his nose again.

Bud loved his new sunglasses. They helped him see better in the glaring desert sun, plus he thought they maybe made him a bit more handsome, but he needed to get some kind of little anti-skid doohickey for them.

They were a gift from his wife, Wilma Jean, who had secretly hoped they would cure Bud's habit of always rubbing the bridge of his nose when he was thinking about something, which, as Sheriff of Emery County, he often was.

Her gift had indeed cured Bud's habit, at least when he was wearing the sunglasses, but he had now developed the habit of fiddling with them.

Watching the sunglasses slowly slide down Bud's nose seemed to drive Wilma Jean even crazier than before. Bud always laughed and told her yeah, crazy with desire, which would make Wilma Jean laugh, but she had to agree that it was better than him smoking, which he'd quit a few years before.

Anyway, apparently Bud was thinking, because he was doing the slow Sisyphean thing with his sunglasses, up, down, up, down. It was an unconscious habit, but it did serve to clue his deputy, Howie, that something was up.

Sometimes that something was something serious, but sometimes it was more along the lines of Bud wondering what was for dinner. Rumor had it that Wilma Jean was a darn good cook, which wouldn't surprise Howie, as Wilma Jean did everything with panache.

Howie knew it did no good to ask Bud what was up, it would just interrupt Bud's train of thought, and then whoever was nearby would get run over by that train, figuratively, at least, and Howie was the only one nearby.

Finally, Bud asked, "Why would anyone want to break into Millie's cafe, tear everything up, and not even take the money in the cash register? It just doesn't make sense. Maybe she's made an enemy somehow, as unlikely as it seems."

Howie replied, "Does Millie even make any money way up there? And why would anyone want to drive clear up on top of the Swell for whatever little bit she does make and not even take it? I agree, no sense at all. Maybe somebody's mad at her."

Bud answered, "That's exactly what I just said, Howie."

Howie had a habit of always agreeing with Bud, which sometimes irritated Bud, as he liked a little back and forth now and then, for it helped him think better, analyze things. But Howie was fairly new to the law-enforcement business, and he didn't want to come across as being argumentative, so he usually just agreed, even when he didn't agree.

Howie had been taught to respect authority, and he had plans to be that authority someday, even though he knew it would take a few years. He wanted to someday be sheriff himself, and that would prove a few things to his ex-wife, for sure. But Howie was smart enough to not tell Bud he was after his job, as he figured Bud wouldn't necessarily encourage that.

Besides, Howie needed a bit more experience, having been a deputy only a few months. Before that, he ran the local drive-through cafe, called, appropriately enough, *Howie's*. He could see it right now, across the street from the sheriff's office, and he wondered how business was going for the new owner. Maybe he'd go get a sandwich there for lunch.

Just then, the phone rang, and Bud answered.

"Sheriff's office, Bud."

A voice on the other end said, "Bud, this is Larry, up at the cafe. Look, you need to get up here ASAP. Somebody or something has torn the place up again, and this time you need to come and actually investigate it, no deputizing me to do it 'cause you don't wanna drive 30 miles. This is gettin' serious, maybe even dangerous."

"Dang it, Larry, what in hellsbell's goin' on up there?" Bud responded curtly. He'd had his mind on going over to the Chow Down for his mid-morning coffee and hated to think of having to drive up on the Swell instead. And that also meant he'd miss lunch with Wilma Jean, and she was making enchiladas, his favorite.

"I dunno, Bud, that's your job, not mine. For cryin' out loud, I'm just a truck driver. I don't have the brains you have for figurin' this stuff out. The kids are sayin' it's some kind of Bigfoot, and we sure don't need any rumors like that. Millie's havin' a hard enough time as it goes without scarin' people away."

Larry paused, then continued, "You just need to get into that old Bronco I helped pay for with my taxes and get yourself up here. You can get a cup of coffee and donut up here. Don't be a crybaby, just come on up."

Bud grimaced. Larry knew him all too well. And the crybaby reference was Larry's revenge for when Bud had called *him* that once. They'd got stuck way out on the Swell looking for wild horses, and Larry had been afraid of the dark. Bud had to admit being scared out there was probably more prudent than not, but he had to admit it only to himself, not to Larry.

Bud grabbed his jacket. He wondered why there was talk about a Bigfoot. The kids Larry was referring to really weren't kids, but instead were geology students staying at the motel up there while working on some project or other. The Swell was always attracting geology and archaeology types, and Bud never really paid much attention to the specifics.

Bud was tired. These last few months, it seemed he was more tired than not. They called it burn-out, he thought.

For a minute he thought of sending Howie up there, but then he remembered that Howie was supposed to go talk to the local Shriners Club about them maybe helping the sheriff's office buy a new vehicle, something Howie would be better at than Bud with that bunch of old goats. Howie was new and still had some enthusiasm, which Bud had long ago lost.

Bud told Howie to cover for him, stepped out of the office and into his old red Bronco, fiddled with the gears (it always stuck a little in reverse), then drove off into the sun, his sunglasses riding on the end of his nose, making him look more like an eccentric accountant than like the Indiana Jones movie star he imagined.

"That's sure a beautiful sight," Bud thought as he drove west on the freeway, the huge white shark's teeth of the San Rafael Reef looming in the distance, an intimidating rock barrier that had once blocked all passage west.

It wasn't until the mid-70s that the Reef had been breached by the new freeway, allowing travelers to go due west from the little town of Green River and connect with Salina, some 110 miles away. The highway department had blasted out Spotted Wolf Canyon to a width that would accommodate the freeway, whereas before it had been less than 20 feet.

Before that, one had to go all the way north to Price, then swing back south through Castle Dale and Emery, skirting the Swell. Now one just jumped on the freeway and zipped up through Spotted Wolf Canyon and presto, was on top, then on down the other side, one of the most scenic drives on earth with its creamy cliffs and rugged canyons.

Bud cruised along as fast as the old Bronco would let him, enjoying the sight of the Reef looming straight ahead. These wild uplifts were called reefs by the early settlers, and rightly so, as that's exactly what they looked like, huge stone reefs hundreds of feet tall and virtually impassible.

He passed the sign that read "No Services for 110 Miles" and thought again about chewing out the highway department for ignoring Millie's cafe and motel on top of the Swell. Weren't those services?

He'd actually called up the highway bigwigs once, and they'd said that services had to include a gas station, or people would assume so and get stuck up there. Bud had thought that might be OK, as Millie could then augment her meager business with gas rescues.

Bud soon topped out on the Oyster Shell Reef, a hill filled with petrified oysters that stretched for miles along the flats below the Reef. The radio crackled. It was Howie.

"Sheriff, I just got another call from Larry, and things are getting serious up at the Ghost Rock Cafe. It appears there's been a murder."

Bud waited for Howie to continue. He didn't, so Bud answered, "10-4, go ahead, Howie."

Howie continued, "Seems someone found a body up there, and that's all I know, Sheriff."

Bud was a little miffed that Howie hadn't gotten more information, but he remembered he was new.

"Do they know who it is? What makes them think it's a murder?"

Howie replied, "I dunno, Sheriff. You want me to call the coroner?"

Bud sighed and said, "Not just yet, let me see what's going on first. And Howie, for the umpteenth time, you can call me Bud anytime you want."

Howie responded, "OK, Sheriff, I just don't want to be disrespectful. My daddy always taught me to be respectful, you know that. Good luck, I'm off to lunch across the street, gotta eat before the Shriner's meeting, but I can come up after that if you want, just let me know."

"Howie, the Shriners always provide lunch at their meetings. I thought you knew that."

Howie answered, "I do know that, Sheriff, but I'm hungry, so I'll eat twice, and that way I won't have to worry about dinner. I can splurge for lunch and it will all even out, since the Shriner's is free. 2-4, I mean 10-4."

Bud put his radio mic back into its holder on the dash and shook his head. It was beginning to seem that Howie had a bit of an obsession with food. He'd need to get over that and watch his weight if he wanted to stay in shape and be in law enforcement.

Bud then reconsidered his craving for donuts and coffee. He'd have to suffer, as enjoying either probably wasn't in the cards now. He then kind of chided himself. What kind of a sheriff was he, thinking about donuts and coffee when some poor person had maybe just been murdered?

He wondered who it was and hoped it wasn't anyone he knew, especially not Millie.

He stepped on the gas a bit as the old Bronco began the torturous climb up through Spotted Wolf Canyon and the Reef and up onto the Swell. He would know soon enough.

2
_____

Bud was soon through the teeth of the Reef and climbing up the Swell. He could now see cattle grazing on the gentle slopes and wondered where the wild horses were. Probably over in Hondu Country, way down on the southern part of the Swell, near Hondu Arch, where they usually hung out.

That's where he and Larry had got stuck that evening, and if it hadn't been for some dirt bikers, they might still be way out there, as it was late November and a storm came in the next day, dropping several feet of snow.

He could now see a rooster tail of dust on a side road that led in from the Swell, and he slowed down a bit, even though he hadn't been going all that fast. He wanted to get a look, see who it was, way out there. It was too early in the season for dirt bikers or the few people that came to explore the slot canyons. He suspected it was the rancher whose cattle he'd seen earlier, probably checking up on them. He wasn't sure who leased the grazing rights up here.

Before long, the dirt road paralleled the freeway, and he saw a gray Dodge Ram pickup. He couldn't quite make out who it was, but he did notice the truck had a brush guard and Utah plates, the old ones with the white background, not the newer ones with the colorful depiction of Delicate Arch.

He could make out two dogs in the back, black and white, probably border collies. Definitely some rancher. The freeway and dirt road soon parted ways, and the pickup was gone, heading in the opposite direction towards Green River.

Bud's radio crackled again.

"Sheriff, I need your advice. Over."

It was Howie.

"Go ahead."

"There's a bunch who's got a whole lot of tents and such set up in the park. Kind of taking the place over. The little kids can't hardly even get to the swings and slide. Any idea what I should do?"

"Howie, it's the Cinco de Mayo folks. Today's their celebration."

"No, Sheriff, can't be them. I hate to disagree, but it must be somebody else. Shouldn't whoever it is have a permit?"

"Why wouldn't it be the Cinco de Mayo people, Howie?"

"Because today's not the cinco. Cinco is Spanish for five. Today's the tenth."

"I know that, Howie, but they postponed it until today because of the weather. It was raining on the fifth."

There was a long pause, and Bud thought maybe he'd lost him.

Finally, Howie continued, "Do they have a permit?"

"No, they don't need one."

"Why not?"

"They're a non-profit."

"Oh."

Bud thought that Howie sounded a bit disappointed.

"Well, OK, over and out."

Bud was soon up on top of the Swell and could see the desert far behind him in his rear-view mirror. Far below, the white Mancos shale shone like a vast sea, which it once had been, long ago.

Ahead, he soon could make out Ghost Rock, a huge buff-colored rock shaped exactly like a ghost, shroud and all. The old-time cowboys had used it as a landmark out in the back country, a way to know where they were when way out chasing cattle. He had seen it on days when the Swell was covered in fog, and it would shimmer and rise above the mists like a huge specter.

Bud shivered and turned on the heater. It was a bit chilly. Days like this, he wished he'd stayed in Radium at his old job as a uranium miner, though now all the mines were closed. Up here, there would be no donuts for him, and none of Wilma Jean's delicious enchiladas.

He'd just have to get Millie to fix him a burger up at the Ghost Rock Cafe, he decided, assuming she was still alive.

He absentmindedly pushed his sunglasses back up the bridge of his nose and drove on.

He was soon at Ghost Rock, the only freeway exit at the top of the Swell. He could see the neon sign flashing off and on, even though it was broad daylight, trying to catch the eye of some hungry or weary traveller. The sign was a replica of the huge rock hovering behind the old motel and cafe, except the sign's ghost had black spooky eyes, unlike the rock.

Bud recognized Larry's big truck cab parked in front of the motel. Larry called the motel home when he wasn't out running loads, as Millie traded him rent for his help maintaining the place, although Bud suspected she mostly just wanted someone around. From the looks of it, Larry hadn't been keeping up his end of the deal for quite some time, Bud noted, looking at the weeds and peeling paint on the buildings. The only other vehicle Bud could see was Millie's ancient baby blue Cadillac. Must be another slow day.

He then noticed a small yellow bus parked over behind the cafe. It had the words *Utah School of Mines* on its side, and *Orogeny Specialists* chalked onto the back window. He then noted the motel's no vacancy sign was on. Maybe business wasn't so bad after all.

He pulled over in front of the dilapidated cafe and got out. He dreaded going inside, as he knew he was in for a difficult task. Murder was rare in this part of Utah, in fact, he had only covered one such crime in his whole stint as sheriff, a good five years, and that turned out to be the work of some out-of-staters who robbed the little gas station in Green River and thought it then necessary to shoot the attendant. That crime had been solved in less than an hour, as the state troopers immediately pulled the two guys over and arrested them.

He paused, held his breath, and pulled on the handle of the glass door with a ghost painted on it. He was still wishing he was down in town, heading for the Chow Down, getting ready to enjoy one of Karen's fresh-baked donuts—back when life was simple, a mere hour ago.

What he saw when he entered the cafe made him feel better, for Millie was sitting in a back booth crying, with Larry next to her, trying to console her. Good, thought Bud, at least she wasn't the object of the murder. He already knew Larry wasn't dead, as he'd been the one to call it in.

But what he saw next made him feel worse—the cafe was in shambles. Several booths had been tumbled onto their sides, a couple of windows had been shattered, and dishes and silverware were strewn across the floor.

The only others in the cafe were two fit-looking young guys dressed in blue jeans, hiking boots, and denim shirts, who were quietly cleaning up the mess. Bud suspected they were some of Larry's "kids," geology students, for they looked to be the right age, early twenties.

Bud was concerned. It looked like they hadn't waited for him to get there to investigate.

"Say," he said. "You fellows leave things alone until I can check it all out. I appreciate you trying to help, but I'll need any clues I can get."

The kids stopped, not sure what to do.

Larry replied, "This isn't where it happened, Bud. It was out at Swasey's cabin. He's still out there."

Bud nodded to the young guys. "OK, carry on."

He then went to where Millie and Larry sat. Millie's dishwater blonde hair was tied back in a pony tail, and she looked tired, her eyes red and swollen. She wore a smudged t-shirt that read, *Rural and Proud*, and she had a green sweater wrapped around her thin shoulders. Larry was next to her, handing her tissues as she cried, looking helpless.

Bud sat down across from the pair, noting Larry's baseball cap du jour, a blue one, with the words *Very Large Array* imprinted upon it. Larry collected caps and always had a new one from his trucking travels, but Bud had no idea what this one meant or where it came from.

He waited for them to tell him what had happened. Millie lifted her head and noticed him, then burst out crying again, kind of a low sad wailing. Larry looked even more helpless, and Bud decided to go get himself a cup of coffee until Millie regained her composure.

He knew the body had to be that of someone Millie knew for her to be this upset, as she was typically very pragmatic and used to dealing with all kinds of trouble and mayhem. He remembered the time she'd called him to come up and straighten out some drunk archaeologists who were tearing the place apart, only to find them passed out in front of the motel, hands tied with dishtowels, when he got there. Millie didn't mess around when she got mad.

Bud went behind the counter and poured himself a cup of coffee, then came back around and sat down at the long bar. He was pouring some creamer into his cup, wondering if the vandalisms and the murder were related, when one of the geology students sat down on the stool next to him.

"Sheriff, I'm Todd. I'm the guy who found him."

"Found who?" Bud asked.

"Isn't that why you're here?" Todd asked in reply.

"If you mean you found the dead person, yes, that's why I'm here. I'm just wondering who it is."

"It was a real bummer, I can tell you that," Todd said quietly.

Bud answered, "Yes, I can imagine it was. Can you tell me a bit more about all this? Where is he, and does anyone know who he is?"

"It's a bit out there. It's gonna take a four-by-four to get there. Maybe a good half-mile from here. I was out hiking, working on our field survey, when I found him."

"Is the body where you found it?"

"Yes, sir, I would never tamper with evidence, even if I had wanted to, which believe me, I didn't. I'll show you how to get there, but I'm not getting out. Once was enough for me. It's not every day you see someone killed by a Bigfoot, and trust me, it's not a pleasant sight."

"A Bigfoot?"

"Yes, sir, several of us have had encounters."

"A Bigfoot." Bud whistled. "OK then," he added, "Let's go."

3

Bud and Todd slowly drove up an old road above the Ghost Rock Cafe, winding back in the juniper and pinion trees at the base of a long cliff that eventually ended at the edge of the deep and spectacular Eagle Canyon.

They were soon at what was known as Swasey's cabin, which looked like it was built long ago and would soon melt back into the earth. The logs were weathered almost white from the sun and elements.

Bud hated what he had to do next, but it was part of his job. He was glad it was a very rare part. Fortunately, murder wasn't a common thing around here, unless the mice and rabbit dinners of the coyotes qualified.

Bud parked the Bronco a ways from the door, as he didn't want to obliterate any possible tracks or other evidence. He carefully looked around the outside of the cabin, taking photos, while Todd sat in the Bronco.

He didn't see anything unusual—until he entered the cabin, that is, and he wasn't prepared for what he did see.

There, on a cot, amidst what looked like a few years' worth of trash and debris, was a body, a body that looked like something had seriously chewed on it. The clothes were in tatters, and whoever it was seemed to have been in the sun a lot, as they were well-tanned, what was left of them, that is.

He examined the body as best he could, then carefully searched the cabin's interior for clues, taking yet more photos.

But he soon had to leave, as it was getting to him, both mentally and physically. He'd had all he could take and was soon back in the Bronco with Todd. They drove back to the cafe, neither saying a word.

Bud was now on the radio, trying to get Howie, who appeared to still be in the Shriner's meeting, because he wasn't responding. This was bad, Bud thought. He was going to have to talk to Howie about what covering for him meant, which was, basically, keeping your radio on and answering it. Since they didn't have a dispatcher, it was up to Howie to keep things going when Bud was gone.

Bud tried again, only this time calling from his cell phone. Maybe Howie was at the office. Sure enough, Bud got through.

"Sheriff's office, Bud," Howie answered.

Bud was surprised, how did Howie know it was him?

"Howie, what's up with the radio? I've been trying to get through."

Howie sounded embarrassed, "Gee, Sheriff, I forgot it, it's in the car. I'll go get it right now."

Bud tried to interrupt, but it was too late. Howie had apparently put the phone down and gone to the car. Bud waited for a bit.

Finally, Howie said, "Sheriff, you want me to hang up so you can radio me? I'll have to go back over to the car. I forgot you can't take those things out. But I've been covering things here at the office, Sheriff, not to worry, I just can't answer the radio."

"No, no, that's OK," Bud answered, trying not to be exasperated. "Howie, just call Doc Richardson. We need a coroner up here. I don't have his cell number with me—it's in my Rolodex. Tell him it's a ways out there, so to try to get here as soon as he can. We don't want to be out there after dark, as there's not much of a road."

Howie was curious, "Who's the victim, Sheriff? And who done it, do you know?"

Bud answered, "It appears to be the Swasey hermit, his first name is Joe. I have no idea who did it, but I intend to find out. Call the doc and see when he can get up here and let me know."

"I'm on it right now, Sheriff," Howie answered, "10-4 and over."

It was a good half hour later that Bud heard Howie calling him on his car radio. Unable to get outside in time, Bud called Howie back on his cell phone.

"No offense, Sheriff, but you should stay by your radio," Howie chided Bud, "In case of an emergency. I finally got ahold of Doctor Richardson, and he's on his way."

"Good, good," Bud replied. "Where's he coming from?"

"I dunno, Sheriff, I thought he lived in Price," Howie answered.

"I know that, Howie," Bud said, trying to be patient. "But his practice covers a big area. Any idea where he was when you called him? He even sees patients in Green River."

"I dunno, Sheriff."

"OK, well, cover for me. I may not be back till after dark. Say, how did the Shriner's meeting go?"

Howie paused for a moment, then answered. "Fine, fine, at least I think so, anyway."

"Any idea if they'll help us get a new vehicle?"

"I dunno, Sheriff. See, I actually didn't make it to the meeting."

"You didn't? Why not?"

"The patrol car broke down."

"Howie, you can walk about anywhere in Green River in less than 10 minutes. Why didn't you just walk to the meeting?"

"I'm sorry, Sheriff. I figured it would be better if I didn't go, it would make the point a lot better than I ever could."

Bud thought about that for a minute, then said, "Good thinking, Howie. You may be right. Where's the car now?"

"It's across the street at Howie's. It actually just has a flat tire, and I'm workin' on it right now. Over and out."

The phone went dead, and Bud shook his head.

"That boy's never gonna make Sheriff of Emery County," he said out loud to himself.

Millie, who had stopped crying and was now making hamburgers, shook her head in agreement while Larry just grinned at the thought.

"I'd make a better detective than that chow hound would, Bud, no offense to Howie, he's a good guy, don't get me wrong, but he just doesn't have the analytic side a good deputy needs. He makes a heck of a good sandwich, though. He should've stayed at his cafe, 'cause that place is going downhill fast."

Millie served Bud and Larry hamburgers, then sat down next to them in the back booth.

She said, "Bud, I understand if you can't talk about it, but now that you've been out there, what do you think happened to Joe? I mean, who or what killed him? He was an eccentric guy, but harmless. He came by here every day, and I gave him a free burger."

Bud asked, "When did you see him last, Millie?"

She answered, "Day before yesterday. I wondered why he didn't come by yesterday. Now I know. You know, I gave him a free meal every day for years, but just lately, he insisted on paying me. I don't know if it means anything or not, just thought I'd mention it. But what happened?"

Bud replied, "I don't know, but it appears Joe was killed by some kind of wild animal. My vote goes for a cougar, but it's just so unusual. I mean, in all my years in this country, I've only been around a cougar once, and that's that night we were stuck out in Hondu Country, so for one to come into a man's camp and actually kill him is about unheard of."

Bud immediately wished he hadn't mentioned Hondu Country to Larry. He knew it would trigger bad memories.

Sure enough, Larry answered, "I'll never forget that night, Bud, and I'll also never forget what a fearless hombre you were out there. I was about to pee my pants and you weren't even scared."

Bud wondered if this would be a good time to tell Larry the truth. He decided it would, to set the matter to rest once and for all.

"Look, Larry, I was scared to death out there, too. I just didn't want you to know it. Fear breeds fear, and we would've both been hopeless basket cases."

Larry looked surprised, but a bit vindicated. He started to say something, but Millie interrupted.

"What the heck happened out there that night, anyway? I can't even get Larry to talk about it."

Bud wasn't sure he wanted to talk about it either, and he now regretted bringing it up, especially in light of the day's event, but Larry now seemed eager to revisit it.

Larry said, "We got stuck out there, right in that cottonwood grove where the road ends at Muddy Creek, right under Hondu Arch. Stucker than a jackrabbit in bentonite gumbo. The more we spun our wheels, the deeper we went. There we sat, prime bait, darker than Hades and cold, too. No survival gear, like the dumb arses we are. We tried everything we could, even put the floor mats under the wheels, then figured we'd have to spend the night and walk out the next day."

He paused, looking at Bud for approval, as he'd never told the story before. Bud was apparently studying something in his coffee cup, so Larry continued.

"We tried to get comfortable, but we knew it was gonna be a long night. Then about seven o'clock, this was November, so it had been dark a couple of hours by then, we heard something howling out in the rocks, and believe me, it was nothing I've ever heard before or since. Then something started rocking my pickup. I looked up and saw a big black head looking at me with eyes that glowed red in the dark. Whatever it was, it was massive, and it wasn't no cougar. I started yelling. Bud never saw it and he didn't believe me."

"I did too believe you, I just didn't want to make things worse," Bud said, still studying his cup, but now fingering the sunglasses in his pocket.

"You called me a crybaby."

"Dang it, I was just trying to defuse things, Larry, make you mad so you'd stop being so scared."

"Well, whatever. I turned on the engine and lights and started honking the horn, and it ran away. Some guys with dirt bikes were getting out late and saw our lights and heard us honking, so they came down off the hill and got us unstuck. Bud helped them load up their trailers, but I was too scared to even get out. I had them follow us out. And I ain't never goin' out in that wild country again. If it weren't for helping Millie, I'd be living down in Price or Elmo right now."

Larry sulked for a minute, then added, "And it sure as hellsbells wasn't no cougar."

Now Todd, who had been sitting alone at the bar, apparently eavesdropping, came over and said, "I've seen it out there myself, and he's right. It's not a cougar. It's a Bigfoot, and I know it killed Joe Swasey. It's damaged the cafe twice now, and we have to do something before it kills someone else."

About that time, Doc Richardson walked in the cafe door. He must've been close by, Bud thought, to get here that fast.

4

Bud sat at the bar in the Ghost Rock Cafe, rubbing the bridge of his nose, engrossed in thought. Doc Richardson had taken Joe's body back to the morgue.

It was getting on towards evening, and he'd just called Wilma Jean to tell her he'd be late coming home tonight.

She was down at the bowling alley, which she owned, and he'd had to leave a message, which he didn't like to do. He didn't want to bother her, as she was probably bowling in the leagues and would get mad if he distracted her, but he wanted to be able to explain things a bit so she wouldn't be irritated.

He was thinking about everything, trying to figure it all out, when Millie came from the kitchen with several pizzas on a tray. Larry was gone, back in his motel room, and the geology bunch had returned from the field and were having dinner. They'd pretty much mended the cafe, taping cardboard over the broken windows and righting the booths. Bud was glad they were here.

It made Bud hungry again, smelling the pizza they were having, even though he'd eaten not too long ago. Maybe he should give it up, go on home, and come back tomorrow. It wasn't too late for those enchiladas. He knew Wilma Jean would've saved him some.

But he was sheriff. That was his job, and certain things went with the territory. Things like thorough investigations. He had to go back out to the cabin. He owed it to Joe Swasey to find out who had killed him, and yes, who, not what. He wasn't so convinced about the Bigfoot idea any more than he was convinced that Bigfoot even existed. It was hard for something mythical to kill you, unless you died of fright from your own imagination.

Bud had tried to deputize Larry, make him go out there with him, but Larry flat out refused, even under threat of contempt and going to jail.

"I'd rather be in jail than in Swasey's old cabin at night," Larry had said. "At least I'd be safe in jail." Bud had to agree. He didn't want to be there at night either, but something was nagging at him.

Bud thought about the evidence he'd collected so far. It wasn't much, just a half-eaten hamburger. He had put it in an evidence bag, and he wondered if you could fingerprint a hamburger. The thing that bothered him was the age of that hamburger, as it wasn't all that old.

If Joe Swasey had last been in the cafe two days ago, that hamburger had to be at least that old, and this one was pretty fresh, a few hours at the most. Millie had said Joe hadn't been into the cafe for two days—but the geology guys had, and she'd made them hamburgers for their sack lunches every day, she'd told him.

He knew how old that burger was based on studies he'd done himself with old hamburgers in his Bronco. He knew exactly how long it took for the bun to get really hard, as well as the hamburger to get crunchy and the pickles to curl up. He was also an expert on old French fries. Wilma Jean was always getting after him for forgetting about his lunch when he got busy, something he guessed Howie never did—forget his lunch *or* get busy.

Bud had also taken lots of photos of the cabin and its surroundings when he'd gone out there with Todd. He felt like he'd been thorough. Doc Richardson had said it was definitely an animal that had killed Joe, but Bud had a nagging feeling in his gut. Something just wasn't right.

He'd seen the body himself, and yes, it looked like an animal had killed Joe, but he was still going to order an autopsy first thing tomorrow, even though the doc had said he was 100 percent sure about the animal attack. But someone could have killed Joe, and then a cougar or something later attacked the body, although that theory really didn't set right with Bud either.

In all his years in the canyon country, his whole life, actually, he'd never seen or heard of anyone attacked by a cougar while in his own cabin, or even out of it, for that matter. Cougars on the Swell were wary because they were hunted by the ranchers, what few cougars there were left, that is. And the Swell didn't have bears, as it was too dry for them.

In fact, the only cougar attack he'd ever heard of was a bow hunter who had smeared himself with deer scent and was wearing green cammies, hiding in the bushes. A young cougar had attacked him and put him in the hospital, but even at that, he'd recovered and lived to tell about it. Young cougars don't know the difference—to them, if it smells like a deer, it *is* a deer.

Bud had personally kind of wondered why the guy hadn't made the Darwin Awards, doing something that stupid, though he never voiced his opinion on that one, since the fellow was one of his constituents.

Maybe Joe had been experimenting with deer scent, thought Bud, but he knew Joe wasn't that crazy. After all, Joe was a Swasey, a descendant of the people who had first ranched on the Swell, and that bunch was as wild, tough, and crazy as any cougar.

Bud wondered if Joe was the great-grandson of the Swasey that Joe and his Dog, the two monoliths over on the other side of the Swell, had been named for. In any case, he knew that Joe was as at home on the Swell as he himself was down at the Chow Down having donuts and coffee, where he wanted to be right this very moment, but couldn't. He tried not to dwell on it.

The geology students, who appeared to be about a dozen in number, were all abuzz with the news of Joe's death, and their professor was now giving them a lecture about staying in their rooms all night, no running around or sitting by a campfire.

Bud wondered how much control their prof really had over them, when a thought came to him. Maybe one of them would come out and sit with him at the cabin. There really was little danger, as he would be well-armed, and he sure would appreciate some company. He really didn't want to be there himself, all alone, but that something was still nagging at him.

He walked over to their table and introduced himself, then asked the geology prof, who introduced himself as Professor Cole, if he could speak with him in private.

Professor Cole was the quintessential geology prof, Bud thought, and looked the part with his plaid shirt, tanned face, worn hiking boots, and faded Levis. A well-hammered rock hammer hung from a holster on his belt.

Bud and Professor Cole sat down at the bar, where Bud answered a few of the prof's questions about the death as best he could, then proceeded to ask a few of his own.

"Professor Cole, where have you guys been all day, and were the students all together, supervised?"

"Well, Sheriff," the prof answered, "We're doing what's called a capstone field course, which is a requirement for graduation in geology. It's intended to bring everything they've learned together in one grand-finale project. What we're doing is walking the outcrops of this area and mapping them. Everyone's been in different areas, and the two you met earlier were assigned the area near the hermit's cabin. In general, we're pretty much together and yet we're not, if you know what I mean. We kind of part ways and then reconnoiter at the end of the day, but we always work in pairs."

Bud thought for a moment, then asked, "Have any of you actually met Joe Swasey?"

Professor Cole answered, "No, not as far as I know."

Bud's next question surprised the prof.

"Professor, do you know, is it possible that there could be any precious minerals in this area, something like gold or silver or anything that one could make money from?"

Bud was thinking of what Millie had said about Joe insisting he pay for his meals. It seems he'd come into some money somehow, and Bud wanted to know how.

The professor thought about it for a bit, then said, "Well, mostly no, as it's not the right formation. But I do know of one instance where silver's been found and even mined, and it's not too far from here. I think it's called Hornsilver Gulch, or something like that. It was probably a small extrusive volcanic plug from the Laramide that had a small bit of silver. But no, in general it's not like Colorado's San Juan Mountains. It's sure not where I'd go looking for precious metals."

Bud nodded his head, wondering what the heck the Laramide was, then asked about having a student hang out with him at Joe's cabin. Professor Cole said that, since Bud was the sheriff, if he deemed it necessary, who was he to interfere with justice? He'd leave it up to the kids to decide for themselves, as long as there was no danger.

Bud had a few pieces of pizza with the students and hobnobbed a bit, asking them about their project, but the upshot of it all amounted to nothing. He had learned nothing new, no one volunteered to help him out, and he would have to go it alone, with no reinforcements.

He stood for a moment outside the cafe door, fingering the sunglasses in his shirt pocket, wishing it were morning already and the night was over. He then got into his old Bronco and slowly and reluctantly began the drive out to Joe Swasey's old cabin, carefully following what there was of a road. The neon lights of the Ghost Rock Cafe and Motel reflected off his red Bronco, then finally faded behind him into the dark night.

5

Bud slowly drove the old road out to Swasey's cabin, not in a hurry to get there, the little change can on his dash rattling a bit. His lights lit up the juniper trees along the road, giving them an eerie glow.

He came around a corner just as something quickly slipped off the road. Hitting his brakes, he wondered what it had been. It was too low to the ground to be a deer and had the tawny color of a cougar, but was too small. Maybe a bobcat, he thought.

He had noticed earlier a small grove of large juniper trees not far from Swasey's cabin, and it was there that he parked his old Bronco, turning it around so as to make a quick getaway if necessary.

He always did that—it was a habit he'd learned as a kid out on patrol when visiting his grandfather, who had been sheriff up north in Carbon County. Bud had never had a mind to go into law enforcement himself and wanted to instead be a farmer, but now here he was anyway, a sheriff.

The Bronco was now pretty well hidden. Bud leaned into the back of the vehicle and took out his heavy jacket and put it on. It would be a cold night. It was still chilly up here on the Swell, and at an elevation of 7,000 feet, it was a lot colder than down in Green River, almost 3,000 feet lower. He subconsciously patted his concealed Ruger, grabbed his big police flashlight, then quietly walked towards the cabin.

He had earlier noticed a large pinion tree that would provide a good lookout spot, close, but not *too* close to the cabin, and he snuggled down into its branches, well-hidden in the needles, his back against the tree trunk. He'd had to break off a few branches to get comfortable, but the tree had a deep bed of dead needles under it, which would provide some warmth and comfort.

Now all there was to do was wait. For some reason, he didn't want to go into the cabin—who *would* want to hang out in there? Joe, like so many old guys, hadn't cared a whit about keeping the place clean, making it hard for Bud to investigate the murder. It was littered with old cans and papers and trash in various states of decay.

Maybe someday an archaeologist would find the remains of the cabin and have a field day, Bud thought. He figured he'd have to come back in the daylight and take another look, but for tonight, he'd just watch and wait—for what, he had no idea.

Now the last vestiges of waning light turned into deep darkness. Like all humans, Bud had poor night vision, and this made him feel helpless. He sat in the blackness, waiting for the moon to rise. He knew it was a half moon and he'd have some light, enough to see what was going on, if anything happened.

He waited in the cold, getting stiff from sitting. The moon finally came up over the distant cliffs, lighting them until they shone like petrified butter in the distance. Bud had always liked the Swell, even though it was a wild place and sometimes made him feel like he was on the very edge of civilization. Sometimes he liked that feeling, sometimes not. Right now, it was more not. He was starting to get cold. He wondered if he could last the night.

Then it happened. Bud stiffened as he watched something coming through the trees from the direction of Eagle Canyon. The gorge was a wild and raw place, beautiful as it was, with access into its depths in only a few places, behind the cabin being one.

Bud watched, again fingering his Ruger. It wasn't a cougar, he could tell that right away, as it was too big and looked to be upright.

Plus, it wasn't a tawny color, but appeared to be dark. It had to be a bear, a rare sight here, and a bear walking upright was even rarer.

He studied it as it came closer. He suddenly had the feeling that he was being watched, that it could see him, and this brought raw terror like cold water into his veins. He could actually feel the hairs on the back of his neck stand up.

He now considered running, but he knew whatever this was could easily outrun him. It had come close enough that he could make out its size, and it was huge—as Larry had said, massive.

He thought of Larry for a moment, then thought he himself might actually start crying, he was that scared. He might have a little crow for dinner next time he saw Larry, assuming he ever did.

The creature stood in the shadows, preventing Bud from getting a good look, then walked to the cabin, lifted the yellow crime tape Bud had placed around the building, opened the door, and entered.

Bud was now in a bit of a shock. Whatever it was, it had to have hands to lift the tape and open the door. It had opened the door, hadn't it? He hadn't hallucinated the whole thing, had he? No, he could see the door hanging open in the moonlight. Maybe it hadn't been latched.

What was it doing in the cabin? Had it come back to dine on Joe? Had it killed Joe, like everyone said, and just what the heck exactly was it? Bud was now chilled to his toes. This would be a good time to run like heck, he thought, while it was inside.

He now realized he was still being watched, but now from inside the cabin. He could make out a massive head looking through a window directly at him. He'd better stand his ground. He had a better chance here with his gun than running with it close behind. He knew instinctively that he could never outrun something that big. He now knew what it felt like to not be the highest on the food chain.

Now the creature was coming back out. It apparently had discovered that Joe was gone. Would it be angry and come after Bud? He was so scared he could barely move, but he managed to take out his Ruger.

Somehow, the thing knew, it had seen the gun, because it

instantly turned and walked away, back towards Eagle Canyon. But just for a moment, it turned back, and what Bud saw and heard he knew would stay with him a long time, haunting his dreams and making it so he would never want to camp alone again.

Its eyes now glowed in the dark, glowed red with their own energy, not a reflection. And those eyes were a good eight feet off the ground. It stood there for a moment, looking back at him, and then it made a moaning howling sound that chilled Bud to his core, turned, and disappeared into the darkness.

Bud sat in shock for some time, then slowly came to his senses. It was time to go, to get the heck out of there.

Just then, he heard the low sound of an engine in the distance, and it wasn't but a moment before he could see a vehicle coming down the road.

6

Bud hunkered back down under the tree, wondering if he was as well hidden as he thought, especially after the bear or whatever it was had managed to see him. The vehicle came on down the road, then turned and stopped right in front of the old cabin.

Whoever it was, thought Bud, they weren't trying to sneak around, other than coming here in the night. They must not expect anyone else to be here, because they weren't being very quiet.

He was just far enough away that he couldn't make out who anyone was, but two people got out of a gray pickup, he could see that much. They talked for a moment, then one lifted the tape and went into the cabin, its door still hanging open. Bud could now see a flashlight being shone all around, like the person was looking for something. He wondered what.

After about five minutes, the person emerged. Now the two were talking loud enough that he could make out voices, but couldn't really hear what they were saying. One of the voices sounded a bit familiar, and he tried to place it, but couldn't.

Now they were back in the truck, turning around and leaving. They apparently hadn't found what they were after, as it didn't look like they were carrying anything other than the flashlight.

Bud wondered, sitting there under the tree, if he was ever going to get his toes warmed back up, and if he could even walk back to his Bronco. At this point, he was just wanting to go home. He'd done his best, and nothing made sense, so maybe it was time for some sleep.

As the truck slowly climbed back up the road, Bud carefully, stealthily, snuck along the bushes back to the Bronco. As much as he wanted to go home, he knew he had to find out more. He needed to follow that truck and see who it was. He had been able to see that it had Utah plates, the white kind, but he couldn't make out the numbers.

He started the Bronco and followed the pickup at a good distance, leaving his lights off, hoping he wouldn't crash and burn into the junipers and pinions, especially with that creature still out here somewhere. In fact, he was still scared stiff and kept thinking he could see red eyes following him in the distance. It truly left him more frightened than anytime in his life, including the mine cave-in he'd been in right before he gave up mining.

His hands and feet were so cold he could barely drive, but he managed to stay a good distance behind the truck until it was finally back at the road that went by the Ghost Rock Cafe.

Bud now pulled over on a little rise where he could see down onto Millie's struggling enterprise. He cut the engine.

The gray truck pulled over in front of the now quiet motel, and its passenger stepped out, pausing as if talking to the driver for a moment, then entered a motel room. Bud made a note of which room it was. He could find out from Millie who was staying there, but he thought he already knew from what he could see in the moonlight.

It looked like Professor Cole.

The pickup now took off, entering the freeway on-ramp, and was soon rolling on down that long stretch along the flanks of the Swell. Bud left his lights off, following, until the pickup disappeared over a small rise, then he turned on his lights and floored the accelerator, hoping he could keep up.

The moonlight lit up the flanks of the cream-colored cliffs that wove along the freeway, and Bud could now see that the pickup was a good quarter-mile ahead of him and accelerating. He would never be able to keep up, and he wished he had that new cruiser he'd been trying to get funding for. But Green River was a small town, maybe 800 people at the most, and money was tight.

He now had the Bronco going top speed and wondered if it was maybe going to soon fall apart, leaving him by the side of the road strapped into the bench seat, just sitting there, as the wheels rolled on down the freeway. At least the vehicle had a good heater, and he was starting to warm up a bit.

The truck was now gone, far ahead, and he thought about calling Howie at home and having him catch it as it came down off the Swell, get a license plate number and see who it was, but he figured by the time Howie answered the phone (if he did) and got going, the truck would be long gone. Bud would then be stuck with an endless barrage of questions, and he was too tired.

He drove on down the Swell, giving up on the idea of catching up with the pickup. Then suddenly, he noticed red tail lights off to the side, on that same dirt road he'd noticed a gray pickup on earlier. Whoever it was had left the freeway and was now on that dirt road going off onto the Swell.

Bud had an idea now, and he thought maybe he'd be able to figure out who it had been up at Swasey's cabin. He would go on home, get some sleep, then figure it all out tomorrow. He was tired, and what he'd seen was still bothering him, those glowing red eyes. He needed sleep.

He finally cruised on into Green River. The little town was pretty dead during the day, and at night it was almost downright depressing. All the neon lights were turned off, and it made everything look a bit ghostly, the little town sleeping out in the middle of that big expanse of white Mancos desert.

He heard a lonesome whistle and watched a long freight train bisect the town, on its way east to the bigger more prosperous towns in Colorado. The train would soon drop into the redrock canyons of the Colorado River, winding its way on through the night.

Bud kind of wished he were on it. He'd ridden the train to Grand

Junction a few times and really enjoyed it. He'd have to do that again soon, he thought, maybe take Wilma Jean on a little junket to do some fine dining and shopping—fine compared to Green River, anyway.

He passed the old blue *Gas Up Here* sign, complete with stars radiating out from the word *Gas*. The station itself was long gone, only a broken cement slab remaining.

Bud liked his little town. There wasn't one stop light, and the people were friendly and good-hearted, even if not particularly well-off. Maybe that went together, shoots, he didn't know.

He turned by the old Presbyterian Church, noting for the umpteenth time that the roof needed some new shingles, then swung across a few blocks over to Long Street, which led out to the big melon farms along the Green River. He and his wife had a nice little bungalow on a couple of acres near town off Long Street on Kings Lane.

Wilma Jean had left the porch light on, which meant she wasn't mad at him. This was good, as maybe she'd saved him some enchiladas. He parked over by the old barn instead of in the driveway so not to wake her up. He figured it was about three a.m., and she'd have to get up early to go open up the Melon Rind Cafe, which she owned, along with the bowling alley.

Wilma Jean was quite the business woman, Bud noted, and that was good, 'cause it meant they had some financial stability, something being sheriff would never bring. Maybe he'd even be able to retire someday.

He quietly opened the back door, glad that their dog, Hopalong, AKA Hoppie, hadn't heard him. He then went into the kitchen, quietly took some enchiladas out of the refrigerator, put them in the microwave, and sat down. It had been a long night, and his toes were still a bit cold.

After eating, he got into his flannel pajamas, ate a handful of antacids, then crawled into bed, where he accidentally put his cold toes against Wilma Jean's bare legs.

She let out a scream in her sleep and whacked him, right in the face.

It was the perfect ending to his day, Bud thought.

He hugged her, turned over and went to sleep.

7

Bud was hot and sweaty, the opposite of what he'd been a few hours before, now dreaming he'd been trapped by a half-bear half-Bigfoot and it was starting to eat him, slobbering all over his face. He moaned and turned over, waking himself.

Hopalong, or Hoppie, their Basset hound, thus named because of a funny little hop in his gait, was licking him in the face, happy to see him, but thinking he'd be happier eating some of Bud's breakfast, if he could just wake him up.

"Dang it, Hoppie, I really need more sleep," Bud complained, though actually glad the dog had awakened him from his bad dream —or maybe Hoppie had caused the bad dream, but either way, the clock said it was after eight a.m., and he needed to get things done, since he was the sheriff.

Wilma Jean was long gone to the Melon Rind Cafe. Sometimes he wondered if he was really married or if she wasn't just a figment of his imagination, albeit a pretty one.

Hoppie was sitting on Wilma Jean's side of the bed, where he had spent the night under the covers at her feet, probably dreaming about being a good watch dog. He always slept there, and Bud wondered how he kept from suffocating. He was wagging his tail, happy that Bud was awake.

Bud got up, took a shower, fed Hoppie what he suspected was his second breakfast of the day, let the dog out into the big shady yard, then got into his Bronco, put on his sunglasses, and headed for the office. Howie would be there covering for him, he hoped.

Sure enough, the old black and white police car with Emery County Sheriff emblazoned on its side sat there, its flat tire repaired. Howie was indeed holding down the fort. He was probably sitting in Bud's big fake-leather chair, reading old *Lost Treasure* magazines he got from the free bin at the library, feet up.

Bud wondered if they might be better off just putting a dummy in the car and setting it at a busy intersection, which is what a little town in Montana did, according to a deputy he'd met once at a conference. It slowed people down, at least until everyone figured it out, and it saved the cost of a deputy.

They could use Howie's salary to buy a new vehicle, he thought, but then decided he wasn't being very kind to Howie. Thinking of Howie and how he would want to know all about what happened yesterday made Bud change his mind about going into the office, and he decided to go get some coffee instead. He sure could use some, as it had been a long traumatic night. He would wake up a bit, then go back to the office and see how things were going.

He pulled into the parking lot of the Chow Down. Its owner, Karen, always chided him about not going to the Melon Rind, since Wilma Jean owned it. Bud had told Karen he needed a neutral place to meet people, where they knew Wilma Jean wouldn't be listening in.

Wilma Jean was always wondering what went on around town, being the self-appointed but unofficial keeper of the town's pulse. The truth was that Karen made fresh donuts every morning and Wilma Jean didn't, as she didn't want to get up early after bowling late almost every night.

Bud parked in front of the cafe, walking over to the door, where he became the object of interest for two black and white border collies in the back of a pickup. They waited until he was right next to them, then barked madly. He jumped, then talked to them until they settled down a bit.

He went on inside and slid into one of the green upholstered booths, nodding at several of the other patrons and taking off his sunglasses. Karen came over, asked where he'd been, then took his order of coffee and a donut—make that two donuts—then he kicked back and looked around the cafe.

Just then, something clicked. He stood back up, went outside and looked at the pickup with the two dogs, who were barking madly at him again. Apparently border collies, smart as they were, had poor memories, or maybe it was because now he wasn't wearing the sunglasses.

Sure enough, it was a gray Dodge Ram pickup with white Utah plates and a brush guard on the front. He thought about last night, wrote the plates down in his little pocket notebook, looked a bit at the dust covering the tailgate, then went back inside.

He sat there, enjoying being back down off the Swell and in the comfort of civilization. Casually looking around, he noticed a man he suspected was the owner of the pickup, an older rancher-looking guy in an off-white and well-worn cowboy hat, wearing an old faded jeans jacket with holes in the elbows over a Western shirt and the ever-ubiquitous Levis.

Bud wondered if the Levis company had ever considered doing a commercial out here in Green River country. They wouldn't have to look for authentic models, that's for sure, as everyone wore Levis, men and women alike.

The man noticed Bud sizing him up and nodded his head, touching the brim of his hat. Bud decided to introduce himself. He grabbed his coffee cup (the donuts were long gone) and went over to the booth where the man was sitting.

"Howdy," he said, "I'm Sheriff Bud Shumway. Mind if I sit down for a minute?"

The man stood, extending his hand. "Jimmy Wilson here. Nice to meet you, Sheriff."

Bud was an avid student of human behavior, and he noted to himself that the guy hadn't exhibited any reluctance to talk to him. He must have a clear conscience, Bud thought. That was a good sign.

"Say, I thought I saw you up on the Swell yesterday. Those your cows up there? Started calving yet?"

"That was probably me you saw, but they ain't my cattle. I'm just over here from Salina helping out my cousin, Henry Tidwell, during calving. You know Henry by chance?"

Bud said he did, for he and Henry went way back. He neglected to add that they went way back to the time he'd arrested Henry for helping himself to a few bales of his neighbor's good alfalfa hay one nice summer night—some fifty or so good bales. But he'd let bygones be bygones, as Henry had made good restitution for it and gone straight after that.

Bud continued, "You been spending much time up on the Swell? We had an incident up there recently, and I'm wondering if you might have seen someone or something suspicious."

"I'm up there night and day, to be honest with you, Sheriff," Jimmy said. "Calving is starting, and it's anybody's guess when they might need a good chaw-chewin' bovine midwife like me. Since Henry works out at the truck stop, I'm helping fill in the gaps. But I can't say I've seen anything suspicious."

Bud noted Jimmy's use of the phrase, "to be honest with you," which, in his experience, usually meant there was more going on than met the eye.

Jimmy's eyes narrowed a bit as he added, "Hang on here a minute. You know, I actually did see something strange. Last night, about two a.m., I saw some guy sitting above the Ghost Rock Cafe, you know that little knoll there, in an old Bronco, with his lights off. I pulled on out, and I'll be darned if he didn't follow me, but I lost him."

Bud was aware that Jimmy knew full-on it had been him in that Bronco. He took a sip of his coffee as Karen came by, doing refills.

"OK, OK," Bud said. "You want to tell me what you and Professor Cole were doing up at Swasey's cabin in the middle of the night?"

"No," Jimmy replied succinctly. "But I will say you're a very sneaky guy, which is a compliment in this context."

"Thanks, but Jimmy, I'm investigating a crime here, and this is serious stuff. One of you knowingly entered a crime scene that was marked no trespassing. I'd sure hate to have to arrest you to get information that you could just as easily provide here over a nice hot cup of coffee. Those cattle might miss you."

Jimmy said nothing for a bit, then replied, "Sheriff, I just can't tell you. I'm not a criminal, and I don't know nothing about nothing. That's all I can say."

"Why can't you say?" Bud asked. He knew his interview was about over, as he could see who was now walking in the door.

"It's illegal for me to talk about it, that's why."

With that, Jimmy said goodbye and left, just as one of Bud's admirers came up to the booth.

It was Professor Krider, a college teacher who had retired in Green River. He wrote murder mysteries as a hobby and was quite successful at it. Apparently Bud was the prof's chosen private consultant, as he always came to him with his questions. The prof had even once followed Bud around all day to see what he did, grist for his books.

"Morning, Sheriff. Let me buy you breakfast, 'cause I'd really like to pick your brain a bit about my latest story. I need some tips."

Bud was still trying to process what Jimmy had just said about it being illegal to talk to him. That was a new one, he thought, inviting the prof to sit down.

He then hoped Howie was doing his job, because the sheriff sure wasn't. He had no idea if he'd ever get back to the office, at this rate.

8

Bud walked into his office, where Howie quickly pulled his feet off Bud's desk and jumped out of Bud's chair, dropping his *True Detective Stories* magazine on the floor.

"Afternoon, Sheriff," he said, standing there nervously. "Just doing some research." He nodded towards the magazine, picking it up. Bud thought Howie was going to salute him, but he didn't.

Bud replied, "It's OK, Howie, you can sit in my chair with your feet on my desk any time you want, as long as I'm not trying to sit there with *my* feet on my desk. Anything new happen?"

Howie relaxed. "Not a thing, Sheriff. I was kind of enjoying being the new sheriff here. I thought maybe you'd resigned."

Bud knew he was trying to kid him, but it still kind of irritated him.

"Howie, you know being sheriff involves a lot more than just sitting around the office and answering the phone. I've been investigating the murder. Anything new?" he asked again.

Howie reported that the Shriners Club had called, wanting to talk to Bud, and Mr. Bentley had thought his car was stolen, but then discovered his wife had borrowed it, and then that new guy Jamie Miller had called again, wanting information on whether or not it was legal to live in one's office, and Howie had referred him to the city, and the Garrison family had called asking them to check on their place once in awhile as they were going on vacation, but nothing new, not really.

Bud was glad. He didn't need any more to think about right now. He had already forgotten to do the one important thing he wanted to do today.

He sat down and dialed the office of Doc Richardson up in Price. He was informed that the doc was busy and would call back. Bud then called Jerry Winslow, the Grand and Exalted Ruler of the Shriners, but he didn't answer.

"Any idea what the Shriners wanted, Howie?" Bud asked.

"Sorry, Sheriff, no idea at all. Probably something to do with a new vehicle."

Bud had already guessed that. "If they call again, get a home number for Jerry, and tell him I'll call him at home tonight."

"10-4, Sheriff. You leaving again? You just got here."

"No, you are, Howie. I was just in the cafe and Willie came by. He needs help catching his horses again, so your assignment is to go help him. You know where he lives, don't you?"

Howie said yes, mumbled something about how he wasn't sure he was cut out to be a cowboy, and walked out the door.

Bud enjoyed having his office to himself for once. He was thinking again about the dummy in the cruiser idea, when the phone rang. It was Jerry of the Shriners.

"Afternoon, Bud. I have some good news for you fellas."

"Go ahead, Jerry, we could use some for a change."

"We're going to buy you guys a new vehicle. God knows you need one."

"That's great, Jerry. In fact, just last night I was involved in a chase and had to give it up 'cause I couldn't keep up. That will really make my job easier."

"Bob Gadd's got an almost new Ford Fiesta he's going to donate. It only has about 150,000 miles on it."

Bud wasn't sure what to say. For some reason, he couldn't picture himself trying to negotiate the numerous high-clearance roads of Emery County in a Ford Fiesta, yet alone chase anyone down.

Jerry started laughing. "Gotcha on that one, Bud. That's a little joke. We're going to give you guys twenty grand and you get whatever you can with that. You can guess who gave most of the money, I'm sure."

No, Bud couldn't guess, but he was appreciative, whoever it was.

Jerry was surprised. "Well, I guess I'll tell you, as he didn't say it was anonymous—Mr. Krider, the retired professor."

Bud had no idea the prof was a Shriner and said so. Jerry replied that Krider wasn't, but he wanted the money to go through them because of the charitable tax benefits, and for Bud to let them know when he'd found a vehicle.

Bud hung up, a bit in shock. Prof Krider was a good guy, and he'd buy him lunch next time he saw him, he decided, pinching himself to make sure he wasn't asleep, because last night was catching up with him fast.

Bud had his feet up on his desk and was reading Howie's *True Detective Stories* and nodding off when the phone rang again. It was Doc Richardson returning his call.

"Doc, I'd like to get another autopsy of Joe Swasey done," Bud said.

The doc was quiet, then said, "It's too late, Bud."

Bud was surprised. "What do you mean, Doc?"

"He was a state ward, Bud, and they just cremated his body. I gave them the go-ahead, since I did the autopsy."

Bud sat there, silent. The state never acted this fast on anything, yet alone someone who had been murdered.

"Who did the cremation?" he asked.

"Nelson's, here in Price. Bud, you know as well as I do that Joe was killed by some kind of animal. You saw him as well as I did. I examined his wounds carefully. He had a big hole in his heart area. I have a lot of experience in these things, and it's irrefutable, it was an animal. As coroner, I did a thorough autopsy, you know that."

"OK, Doc, I respect your opinion, so it looks like I'll have to close the case. Could you send me a copy of your coroner's report?"

Doc said he would, wished Bud well, and hung up.

Bud looked up Nelson's Mortuary and dialed the number. Yes, they had cremated the body this morning. Bud told them he wanted the ashes. He would be up there in an hour or so to get them. Were they 100 percent sure they had the right ashes? They were not to be released to anyone else. And they were also not to reveal where the ashes had gone, under threat of compromising an investigation. He wanted to seal the whole thing, under sheriff's orders. He hung up, hoping he'd got his point across.

Bud left Howie a note, put on his sunglasses, and headed out the door. He really wasn't interested in going to Price right now, as he would much rather be taking a nap at home, Hoppie at his feet, but he needed to get those ashes. They were about the only evidence he had, and he couldn't compromise that.

He was the sheriff, and he knew Joe had been murdered. Everyone else seemed to think a cougar or Bigfoot had killed him, but he had a nagging feeling that somehow that hadn't been the case, and he was determined to figure it all out.

9

Bud had picked up Joe's ashes and hadn't been on the way home from Price for more than ten minutes when he got a radio call from Howie.

"Sheriff, Doctor Richardson up in Price wants you to call him. He says it's urgent."

"OK, did he say what it was about?" Bud asked.

"No, but we caught those horses OK. I guess I make a pretty good cowboy after all. I'm about ready to shut down and go home for the night."

"You go ahead and do that, Howie. I should be back myself in less than an hour, then I'm going home, too. I'm tired and would like to make sure I still have a wife. 10-4, over."

Bud dialed Doc Richardson on his cell phone, wondering what was up.

"Hello, Bud." The doctor had apparently recognized his cell number on his caller ID. "I understand you just came and got Joe's ashes."

Bud was miffed at the mortuary, but he realized that, as coroner, Doc Richardson saw these people all the time and probably had a better relationship with them than he did. Doc had obviously pulled rank on him.

"That's right, Doc."

"Where you at now, Bud? I'd like to meet you and get them back. Seems some of the family would like to have them to spread somewhere out on the Swell."

Bud hadn't expected this, but there wasn't much he could do about it. He didn't want to make a fuss and let Doc know he was still thinking Joe had been murdered. Call it politics, he thought, but he had to work with Doc and needed to keep a good relationship going.

"I'm about 10 miles south of town right now. I'll pull over and wait for you at the turnoff to the Sunnyside Mine."

Doc Richardson was driving a big black Land Rover, and Bud fantasized for a minute about buying one for his next sheriff's vehicle, though he knew he couldn't afford it. But somehow the deputies, all four of them, at the little mining town of Sunnyside had managed to have Land Rovers, each a different color.

But Bud had also heard that Sunnyside was struggling and was getting ready to make some deep budget cuts. Maybe they'd have some used Land Rovers for sale soon.

The doc pulled over next to Bud's old Bronco, and Bud handed him the urn containing Joe's ashes.

"Sorry to put you out like this, Bud," Doc apologized. "I had no idea anyone would want his ashes. Guess he has some distant family."

"It's OK, Doc," Bud answered. "I was actually going to just take them up on the Swell myself and spread them somewhere I knew Joe liked. Didn't figure anyone else cared, so thought I'd do the favor."

He wondered if the mortuary people had told Doc about Bud's orders to not release any information, but he figured Doc knew. He tried to cover a bit.

"I didn't want the mortuary folks to let out that the sheriff was such a soft touch."

Doc smiled. "It's OK, Bud. We all know that, and we know it makes for a darn good sheriff. There's a reason you got re-elected."

Doc towered over Bud in his big Land Rover, and Bud felt thoroughly diminished, even though he was a good foot taller than the doc when they were standing on the ground. He now noticed that Doc had several round bruises on the hand hanging out the vehicle's window. It looked like a shotgun or close-range BB gun wound.

Doc noticed Bud's interest and said, "My wife got a new parrot and the darn thing doesn't like me very well, even though I'm the one who paid for it—over a thousand dollars, too. Every time I try to hold it, it pecks me. Hard, too."

"I bet that hurt," Bud offered. "Both literally and financially." He remembered Doc's wife, Joanne, as she used to occasionally accompany Doc on his trips to the clinic in Green River. She and Doc were the epitome of the adage that opposites attract. Doc was soft-spoken and humble, and Joanne was loud and kind of abrasive.

"Well, Doc, I gotta get home and see if Wilma Jean's made anything for dinner. I haven't seen her for a couple of days."

"Tell her hello for me, Bud. I'll never forget that time I was staying down there for a few days and she ended up getting me to bowl in her leagues. I don't recall ever having so much fun. I tried to get Joanne to join me in leagues in Price, but she wasn't interested. Well, good seeing you."

Doc turned around and headed back to Price, the urn holding Joe's ashes resting on his passenger seat. Bud sat there by the highway for a minute, watching the big coal trucks fly by, then pulled out onto the highway and headed back to Green River, the little change can on his dash rattling a bit, even though it now held a sample of Joe's ashes.

Bud pulled into his driveway and parked next to the house, while Hoppie barked madly. Bud had never figured out if the dog was glad to see him or had forgotten who he was. He loved Hoppie, but Bassets weren't always the brightest bulbs in the socket.

Wilma Jean was home. He knew this because her pink Lincoln Continental was parked right smack where he needed to go through the gate. He'd have to walk around to the front.

She spotted him and yelled, "Honey, could you turn off the sprinklers?" Bud obliged, getting sprayed in the process, then went inside, Hoppie at his heels.

Bless her heart, he thought, his wonderful wife had made meatloaf. He could smell it in the oven cooking.

Wilma Jean patted him on the rear while rushing by. "Hon, I'm on my way to leagues, but dinner's in the oven, give it about 20 more minutes. Meatloaf and scalloped potatoes. How you been, anyway? Remember me?" She laughed and was gone.

Bud was exhausted and didn't mind having the evening to himself. He and Hoppie would have dinner, maybe watch some TV, then go to bed early. He washed up and got into his flannel PJs and slippers. No way was he answering the phone tonight. Howie was on call and could handle things.

He got his dinner from the oven, made himself and Hoppie each a plate, then set down in his big lounger, ate dinner, then kicked back.

Next thing Bud knew, he was waking in his big chair, trying to figure out where he was. Hoppie was whining.

It took Bud a minute, but he finally woke up and realized he'd been dreaming. He shivered, got up and closed the curtains, noting it was almost ten o'clock. Wilma Jean would be home soon, and he would be glad when she got here.

Bud had dreamed that he was camping with Joe Swasey, way up on the Swell near Eagle Canyon, and he'd had to get up to go relieve himself.

They were camped behind some rocks, and it was a really black night. Bud couldn't see a thing.

After relieving himself, Bud started back to his tent, but he could now hear Joe calling him, but from the wrong direction, away from camp. Bud thought this was strange, as he knew Joe had been sleeping next to the fire when he'd gotten up. He stood there for awhile and waited, wondering what was up.

Soon, he could hear Joe's voice again, calling him. No mistake, it was Joe, and it was clear as a bell.

Now Bud called back and started walking out towards Joe's voice. This went on for a bit, and the voice would sometimes change direction, but it was definitely Joe calling him, in distress.

Suddenly, out of nowhere, someone grabbed him, and Bud nearly jumped out of his skin, spinning around.

It was Joe, his long scruffy hair in his eyes, standing there, dead serious, and now Bud was disoriented and scared.

He asked, "What are you doing here, Joe? I heard you calling way out there."

Joe answered, "It wasn't me."

They stood there, looking at each other, and Bud could see fear in Joe's face. Then they heard the voice again, calling, calling.

Joe whispered, "Let's get back to camp, now!"

Back at camp, Joe told Bud how this went on a lot out on the Swell. People would get called away by familiar voices and never come back.

Just then, Bud saw two red eyes glowing in the dark on the other side of the fire. A huge black creature stepped around and went for Joe, who yelled out, but now the creature had him and was dragging him away.

Bud pulled out his gun, and the beast turned and ran.

Joe fell to the ground, telling Bud, "Get the doc."

"But you're not even hurt, Joe," Bud replied, incredulously.

Joe answered, "Bud, I may not be dead, but get the doc."

Joe then turned and faded into a ghost with black spooky eyes, just like the one on Millie's cafe door.

Bud had awakened in a cold sweat.

Just then, he heard Wilma Jean pull up. He was never so glad to see her in his life.

10

"Howie, I'm working at home this morning, then I'll be up on the Swell for the rest of the day. Cover for me."

Howie replied, "Roger, Sheriff," thinking this was exactly why he wanted to be sheriff someday. He would love to work from home.

Howie hung up the phone, then sat down in Bud's big office chair and kicked his feet up on Bud's desk, pulling out an issue of *Desert Magazine*, opening it to an article called *The Dangerous Search for Gold in the Superstitions*.

Bud likewise sat down in his big recliner at home, pulling out his little digital camera and hooking it up to his laptop. He couldn't believe this was the first chance he'd had to look at the photos he'd taken day before yesterday at Swasey's cabin.

Hoppie lay on Bud's feet, snoring, his long ears covering his eyes. He loved it when Bud worked at home. Wilma Jean had told Bud she was getting another dog to keep Hoppie company, but she was waiting for the animal shelter to call her with the right one. It had to be another Basset hound, although a beagle would also be fine. Or a mix of either. Or maybe even a blue heeler. Bud suspected she would take whatever came along.

Bud paused for a minute, thinking about what kind of patrol

vehicle to get. He sure liked the idea of getting something like a new Toyota Land Cruiser, but they were just too expensive. A good reliable vehicle would pay for itself in repairs, but that didn't matter if you didn't have the money to buy one in the first place.

He turned back to the photos, which were now uploading onto his computer. He grimaced when a few showing Joe's torn body came across the screen, but the majority were of the cabin's interior.

Now he scanned through them one by one, making them full size. He studied the ones of the cabin, both inside and out. He had no idea what he was looking for, he just knew it was part of the job of being thorough. He was sheriff, and that meant thorough.

Now he stopped, coming to a photo of the hamburger where he'd first found it. It had been kind of kicked up under Joe's cot, and he'd noticed it only because he was trying not to look at Joe and was wondering where Joe's left boot had gone to, as it wasn't on his foot. Bud had looked around the cabin for that boot without luck, and he wondered if that was a clue of some kind.

That hamburger was now at the lab in Salt Lake City, where they were testing it and looking for fingerprints. He wondered if the lab had ever tested a hamburger before.

Bud scanned to another photo. Most of them were like looking at tornado damage, there was so much junk everywhere. Bud had neglected to go through it all, and he really didn't think he'd find much anyway, as it all appeared to have been deposited long before the murder.

Now something caught his eye, something he hadn't noticed when he was up there. There, hanging directly above Joe's cot, was a small picture of an old Fremont Indian pot, an oil painting that actually was quite well done. Bud was surprised he hadn't seen it when he was there, as it stuck out like a sore thumb among all the drabness and trash everywhere else. He guessed he'd been trying too hard to avoid looking at Joe's body, and the painting was right above Joe's head.

Bud studied it for awhile, wondering what had possessed Joe to have something so nice in such a junky place—and where did it come from, he wondered. He enlarged it a bit and tried to read the artist's signature.

Joe Swasey

What the heck? He had no idea Joe was an artist. Maybe it had been painted by his great-grandfather, the original Joe Swasey. If so, where in heck did his great-grandpa get oil paints way back then? Not up on the Swell. Bud had no idea, but if Joe was that good of an artist, it would explain where he'd been getting his money to buy his own lunches from Millie.

Bud quickly scanned through everything one more time when he suddenly noticed something else that he hadn't seen before. He'd taken a photo of Joe's body from the foot of the cot, and now, for the first time, he noted that the body wasn't square with the cot, but was at a bit of an angle with Joe's left arm actually dangling off. Bud looked at that photo for a long time, then decided nobody would intentionally lie down like that.

Of course, if Joe had been trying to escape a wild animal, that begged another question—why was Joe in bed in the first place? Nobody in their right mind would be in bed when they were trying to fight or escape a wild animal attack. Joe would be on the floor, or even outside the cabin, not on his cot.

Maybe he'd gone there to die after being mortally injured—that would explain it, Bud thought. But to Bud, it just felt off, as if someone had placed Joe there after he'd died. And again, where was the missing boot? Had it fallen off when the murderer was moving Joe and been lost?

Now Bud began going through exterior photos, and he soon found another one that caught his eye. There, on the ground directly under Joe's window, was a huge footprint, one that looked like a bare human foot with five toes, only twice the size of a large man's print.

Bud knew he hadn't intentionally taken a photo of this, because he was seeing it for the first time just now. He must have been trying to photograph something else, or maybe just the perimeter of the cabin in general. But there it was, and it looked to him like it would fit exactly the same size as the weird creature he'd seen up there the other night.

Now, for the first time in over five years, Bud reconsidered being sheriff. Maybe it was time to find another job, maybe get into coal mining up by Price. Or maybe he could grow some melons on their little acreage here and make some money that way. Hadn't he noticed a gas station for sale the other day over on Green River Avenue?

He sat back, noticing he was hyperventilating. He put the computer away, got up, and made himself some coffee. Maybe today would be a good day to go to the office and do some paperwork, rather than going up on the Swell.

He turned on the TV and watched a few minutes of some inane game show where the contestants had to guess what kind of plastic surgery someone had, then turned it off and sat there, drinking his coffee while Hoppie slept.

There was more going on here than Bud could figure, but he still knew deep inside that Joe had been murdered. It seemed like everyone else had accepted the cougar theory, but Bud knew better. He had barely known the old hermit, but he did know he owed him justice.

Bud shared a bit of yesterday's meatloaf with Hoppie, grabbed his camera and gun, and headed up to the Swell. He needed to talk to a few people up there.

He didn't notice that he'd forgotten his sunglasses until he stopped by the post office to express mail a small package containing the sample of Joe's ashes to the lab in Salt Lake City.

11

Bud sat in the back booth at the Ghost Rock Cafe with Larry, eating crow for lunch—well, not literally, as Millie would have never stood for that, with her love of ravens, which are part of the corvid family, same as crows.

There were typically several ravens hanging around outside the cafe where Millie fed them scraps. They seemed to love Millie and would sometimes even eat out of her hand. She was very attached to them. She called them "her birds" and even had names for them, like Quoth, Broken Feather, and the Cisco Kid.

No, the crow Bud was eating looked a lot more like a Bigfoot than like a crow. He was trying to describe to Larry what he'd seen that night at Swasey's cabin and see if it matched with what Larry had seen down at Hondu Arch. Unfortunately, it did.

A group of geology students were in the front booth, arguing about something, and Bud wondered why they weren't out in the field, as it was mid-day. He hadn't seen Professor Cole around anywhere.

Now they were getting a bit out of hand. Bud and Larry stopped talking and listened.

"Look," one of them said heatedly. "Everyone who knows anything knows the Moab Tongue isn't Entrada anymore, it's Curtis. And same with Dewey Bridge Member, it's not Entrada neither, it's Carmel."

"Since when?" another asked.

"I dunno, since anybody who knows anything figured it out. Some prof back a few years ago. Doctor Cole would know."

So, Professor Cole had a Ph.D., Bud noted. He had wondered. All they needed was another doctor around the place, Bud mused, still a bit miffed at Doc Richardson.

A third chimed in, "That means the Entrada only has one member, the Slick Rock. How can a formation only have one member? Are we supposed to call it Entrada or Slick Rock?"

Leave it up to geologists to argue about such things, Bud thought. He knew what the Entrada Formation was from his days in Radium, where it formed the beautiful nearby redrock that was full of arches. Other than that, his geology knowledge was a bit lacking, although he had taken a course on soils from the Utah State Extension Service, which was a bit more pertinent to his field of law enforcement and detective work. He was thinking about growing melons someday, when he retired, so he'd killed two birds with one stone—but Millie wouldn't like him using that expression, he thought.

Speaking of Millie, she'd come out of the kitchen to see what was going on.

"Kids, no need to argue, everyone's A-OK in the Ghost Rock Cafe."

They all laughed and lowered their voices.

Bud decided to go talk to them.

"Anyone know where Prof. Cole is?" he asked.

"He's off with some colleague doing some field work," one offered. "It's our off-day. He works with us five days on and two off, and he does consulting work in his free time."

"What kind of consulting work?" Bud asked.

"Geology," answered a red-headed lanky kid. Bud wondered if he weren't maybe related to Howie, with his savvy answers.

"He does a lot of work for the oil companies," a red-headed girl answered. She looked a lot like the red-headed boy, and Bud wondered if they weren't siblings. She was probably the smarter one in the family.

"How long you kids been up here, and how long you staying?" Bud asked.

The girl answered again, "We've been here five weeks and have one to go. We're mapping the Swell. It's our last class, then we all graduate."

"That sounds like a big project," Bud said.

"It is," she answered. "But we're just doing this upper portion."

"Have you found anything interesting?"

"Oh man, tons of stuff," answered another kid. "Rock art, some cool old cowboy stuff, a couple of rattlesnakes..."

Bud didn't like that last news, as he hadn't heard much about rattlers up here. He thought it was too high for them, but maybe not.

"What kind of cowboy stuff?" Bud asked.

"Some old tin cans, a couple of uranium marker stakes, that kind of thing."

"Anybody see any old boots or stuff like that?" Bud asked. These kids were all over the place, maybe they'd seen Joe's missing boot.

"I found an old boot over by that old cabin," a serious-looking guy offered, adding, "Along with some other stuff."

He appeared to be older than the others. Maybe he was working on a second degree or was a late starter, Bud thought.

Just then, it sank into Bud's consciousness what he'd just said. Bud started rubbing the bridge of his nose.

"Is it still over there?" Bud asked.

"Far as I know," the student answered.

"Can you show me exactly where?" Bud asked.

"Sure, but it isn't anything you'd want to keep. It's all chewed up."

They were soon on their way.

"This is a pretty cool rig," said Roger, the older student who had found the boot, admiring Bud's old Bronco as they bounced up the road to Swasey's cabin, the change can on the dash rattling. "I like the way you managed to get the light bar on the roof without drilling any holes."

Bud answered, "You're the first person who has ever noticed that. I was pretty proud of myself, 'cause now you can take it off and the Bronco's just like it was."

Bud had wired the light bar onto the roof, using the interior walls to anchor it. He added, "And I use a magnetic sign for the sheriff's logo, so that can come off, too."

"Good thinking," Roger said. "This old rig's a collectible. Where's the siren?"

Bud pulled a small horn-like thing off the floor that was connected to his cigarette lighter. "I just hang this out the window," he said sheepishly. "It's not very loud. But we're getting a new rig soon. We just got the funding."

Roger answered, "I wouldn't mind buying this from you when you do, if the price is right. I've always wanted an old Bronco—but remember, I'm a student, so it can't be too expensive."

"Trust me, it won't be," Bud answered. "I might even pay you to take it."

They were now at the old cabin. Bud had been wanting to come back out here, and he was glad Roger was with him. For some reason he didn't feel comfortable out here alone.

He noticed his yellow police tape was still around the outside of the cabin, warning people to stay out, as it was a crime scene.

Roger took him to the old boot. It was back behind a rock cliff that flanked the cabin, maybe fifty feet away.

"Wow, you have good eyes to spot this," Bud commended him. The boot was among some wild holly bushes, almost hidden. The holly, also called Fremont mahonia, was ready to bloom, and a few yellow blossoms were already out.

"That's not where I found it," Roger replied. "I threw it over there. It was originally over here." He pointed to an alcove in the rocks that Bud hadn't noticed before because it was in the shade.

Bud picked up the boot and examined it. It was definitely chewed up, but a careful look revealed whatever had done it didn't have particularly large teeth. Not like a cougar or Bigfoot, but more like a dog or coyote.

It was a brown leather boot, what was left of it, a man's ranch boot, kind of a like a cowboy boot but with flat heels, making it easier to walk. Bud looked inside at the label. *Corral Boots, Leon, Mexico.* He'd heard of Corral Boots, they were very well made and lasted forever—and were expensive.

Bud put the boot in the small pack he carried, noting it didn't appear to have any blood on it. He'd check it out when he got home, maybe send it off to the lab.

Roger looked at him, curious. "You're keeping it?"

Bud replied, "Never know when you might need a spare—it's my size."

They walked over to the alcove.

"Can you show me exactly where the boot was?" he asked Roger.

"Right here." He pointed to the ground, maybe ten feet from the alcove, which was draped in shadows.

Bud walked around a bit, looking for tracks, but found nothing, as the ground was covered with soft detritus from nearby scrub oak. He peered into the shadows of the alcove, but it was too dark to see much. It appeared to go back into the cliff a good fifteen feet or so and had an impenetrable-looking hedge of wild holly growing in front of it.

Roger said, "This place is kind of creepy for some reason. I can't imagine living out here."

"Me, neither," Bud answered, thinking for a moment of his own cozy bungalow. This led to him wondering what Hoppie was doing, if he was digging holes in Wilma Jean's garden beds.

He took his big police flashlight from his pack and began pushing through the holly, the thorns poking at him. Roger helped, trying to hold the bushes back enough that Bud could slip through.

Bud now stood in the alcove, letting his eyes adjust to the dark for a moment.

What he saw next gave him the cold chills. A large black creature sat looking at him, and its eyes reflected red in the glare of his flashlight.

12

Bud was, as they say, frozen in fear, for the first time in his life. He tried to go for his gun, but he literally couldn't move. He had no idea how long he stood there, but now he could hear Roger outside the alcove, asking if he was OK, and he couldn't even move his mouth to answer.

He just stood there, and the creature just sat there, staring at him.

After what felt like an eon or two to Bud, he began to feel the uncontrollable urge to rub the bridge of his nose. He finally couldn't control it, and he moved, breaking the spell.

The creature didn't move, however, and just sat there.

Bud now knew it wasn't alive. It was either dead or a costume. His vote went for the latter. He carefully moved towards it, and it still didn't move. Soon Bud was examining it, and he got out his pocket knife and cut off a bit of hair, sticking it in his shirt pocket.

He stood back, shining his light around the alcove. An art easel! And what looked like frames and canvas and other supplies, all neatly placed on an old upside-down rusted cattle trough.

Bud shone his light on the creature again. It was a good costume, he thought, very well done, and had been propped up on an old saddle tree. He couldn't help but feel irritated that he'd suckered for it.

He noticed a large stick behind it and went around where he could see it better. The stick was attached to a large carved wooden foot, exactly like the track he'd found by the cabin.

Now that he was behind the suit, Bud could see wires coming from the eyes area of the costume and into a battery pack. A costume like this would cost a good chunk of change, he thought.

He yelled out to Roger, "Not much in here, coming out in a minute."

He didn't want anyone else to know what he'd found. It would be his secret for awhile. He took his little digital camera out and quickly took a series of photos of the costume and the interior of the alcove, then pushed his way back through the holly into the sunlight. He wondered if there were some way he could upchuck all that crow he'd eaten earlier with Larry, 'cause it was now becoming indigestible.

The bright sunlight made Bud stumble. He wished he hadn't forgotten his sunglasses.

"Dark in there," Bud said, trying to sound nonchalant.

"I know," Roger replied.

"You been in there?" Bud asked, trying to be all casual.

"I have," Roger answered.

"Why didn't you tell me about the suit?"

"What suit?"

Now Bud felt like a fool. He didn't want anyone to know he'd found the Bigfoot, yet he'd just told Roger. Some detective he was.

"There's a gorilla suit in there. It's been modified to look like a Bigfoot."

"No way!" Roger said. Before Bud could stop him, he was pushing his way through the holly into the alcove.

"Holy macaroni!" Roger exclaimed, soon emerging from the alcove. "Dang scary. I wonder if this is the Bigfoot everyone's talking about, the one Todd saw."

"Of course it is," Bud replied. "You don't think there's two of them out here, do you?"

"Probably not. I wonder why it wasn't here yesterday. And I wonder what happened to the paintings."

Bud's senses heightened. "What paintings?"

"I was over here trying to get the strike and dip of this outcropping when I found this alcove. I was trying to stay away from the cabin, as I knew it had the police tape around it, plus I'm not into dead people and all. I found this alcove, and since I'm a curious guy, I went in. I had no idea it had all this stuff in it. It had a couple of paintings sitting on that old tank by those art supplies. They were really nice."

"What did they look like?" Bud asked.

"They were similar to the pictures Millie had in the cafe, the ones stolen in the break-in. Fremont pots and wildflowers."

This is what Howie must feel like, Bud thought, when he's the last one to figure something out.

He sighed, rubbing the bridge of his nose. He had no idea anything had been stolen from the cafe. Maybe he needed to be a bit more thorough, since he was sheriff. Come to think of it, he'd been so busy with the murder, he hadn't even really investigated the break-in. He needed another deputy, one that was a thinker, he thought.

"Roger, have you mentioned any of this to anyone?"

"No."

"Do you mind if I ask exactly how old you are?" Bud asked.

"Thirty-two," Roger answered.

"Do you know anything about law enforcement?"

"My mom's cousin worked for the police for a few years, doing their filing."

"Roger, as Sheriff of Emery County, I am hereby deputizing you. We'll skip the swearing in. You work for me now, and I'll make sure you get paid, even if it's just a good discount on an old Bronco. But that means you are now legally a law enforcement officer. Everything you saw here and that we discussed is evidence in a possible murder case. You're not to discuss it with anyone but me, nor are you to tell anyone you're now a deputy."

Roger looked impressed. "You mean I'm now a deputy?"

"Yes," Bud answered, "You are now a deputy. But don't forget you're an unarmed deputy, and don't abuse your powers."

"I won't," he said solemnly. "But you have to know, I'm not unarmed. I'm legal to carry concealed."

Bud was surprised. "You are? Why?"

"I'm afraid of cougars," he answered. "I carry a little .22 pistol."

"Well, that would only slow a cougar down a bit," Bud said thoughtfully, "and it wouldn't even phase a Bigfoot. It would be like a gnat bite." He paused. "Well, try not to use it on anybody unless it's in self-defense. I don't have a jail."

"Don't worry," Roger answered. "But I need a badge."

"You're undercover, and don't forget that."

"I won't," Roger smiled. "Even though I got too much geology cluttering up my brain to remember much of anything."

"I want to make one more stop," Bud told Roger, walking over to the cabin and ducking under the police tape. He opened the creaky door and went in, his eyes taking awhile to adjust to the dark.

Roger was behind him, and said, "Wow, what a disaster."

Bud replied, "Yeah, no woman around to clean up after him."

He thought of Wilma Jean. She never cleaned up after Bud, she made him toe the line himself.

"The guy was a real packrat, wasn't he?" Roger commented.

Just then, Bud saw what he needed to know. The oil painting of the Fremont pot was gone.

Bud was now forming a hunch as to why Joe had been killed, but at this point, it was still just a hunch. The pieces didn't even fit together crooked, yet alone right. And he was still no closer to a whodunnit.

13

Bud and Roger pulled up in front of the Ghost Rock Cafe, where Millie sat outside on a big rock, feeding her ravens.

Two of the birds sat in the branches of a large juniper tree above her, and a third inched sideways towards what looked like a piece of cheese, as if sneaking up on it.

It got close enough to grab the cheese and went for it, but instead of grabbing it, hopped up a bit into the air and retreated, as if worried about a trap.

"Silly bird," Millie chided it.

Finally, the bird lunged for the cheese, grabbing it in its beak. But instead of flying off, it dropped the cheese, casually pecked it into several smaller pieces, then stuffed each piece, one by one, into its craw.

It then looked at Millie, who threw it another piece while calling it a pig. The bird now saw Bud and Roger and flew away, snatching the cheese before it went.

"How's the investigation going, Bud?" she asked.

"I dunno," he answered. "I keep thinking of Joe and wondering why anyone would want him dead."

"Joe?" Millie replied. "You sound like you're not buying into the cougar theory." She threw out another piece of cheese. "And you know what? I'm not either."

She stood and wiped her hands on her faded jeans, then sat back down, patting the rock next to where she sat. "You fellas come on over and let's talk."

Bud sat down by Millie as the other two birds flew off. "That's Quoth and Broken Feather, they're mates. The other was the Cisco Kid, their kid from last spring. They know I'm OK, but they don't trust anyone else. They're smart," Millie said admiringly.

"They're cool birds," Bud replied. "Millie, I've been so busy I haven't had a chance to ask you about the break-ins here at the cafe. By the way, this is Roger."

"Oh, I know Roger," she replied, motioning for him to come and sit down also. "It's OK, Bud, I understand you're busy. But the insurance adjuster is coming up tomorrow, so maybe he can call you or something if you don't have a report written up by then."

Bud was surprised Millie had insurance on the place.

"Maybe you'd better tell me about what happened, so I can write it up."

"Not much to tell. The first time, it was just a broken window and glass all over. Larry was here, he said he called you and you had him take some photos and check it out. It was weird, 'cause one of the kids found a big track under the window."

"Did anyone get a photo of it?"

"I don't think so."

"What kind of track?"

"They all said a Bigfoot."

"And the second time?"

"That time someone actually broke in. They trashed the place, but the kids were real good about helping me clean it up. Two broken windows this time. They turned some booths over and threw some dishes and stuff on the floor. Made a big mess. You got here at the tail-end of the cleanup."

"Any more tracks?"

"No, not that I saw, anyway. Larry didn't mention anything."

"What time was the break-in?"

"Well, the first one, I dunno, just sometime in the night. But the second one, it was sometime after midnight, because I had forgotten to turn off the pizza oven, so I came back over after watching the *What's Up Tonight Show*."

"Larry said they didn't take any money. Was anything stolen?"

"Yes, and I'd rather they took the money. Money comes and goes, but Joe's paintings can never be replaced, now that he's gone."

Bud began rubbing his finger along the bridge of his nose. "How many paintings?"

"Two. They were beautiful. Fremont pots. Resting on rocks. One had red Indian paintbrush around it. Joe gave them to me. He said he wanted me to have them, as I'd been so good to him. I had no idea he had such talent."

"Was he selling his paintings? Is that where he was getting his money, do you think?"

"I imagine that was it, though I really don't know. How he would get them into town to sell them I don't know, unless someone was helping him. He didn't have a car."

"Did you ever see anyone up here?" Roger asked.

Millie turned to him. "Not really, just customers. I can see anyone who goes up to the cabin, since the road runs right by here, and nobody ever goes up there. Joe really was a hermit. He didn't like people. He'd just been alone too long up here. He developed a taste for solitude, or maybe he was already that way, I don't know. It kind of runs in the Swasey line, being loners."

"How so?" Roger asked.

Bud answered, "There are lots of stories about the Swaseys around here. They were the first whites on the Swell. Cowboys, cattlemen mostly. They discovered a lot of stuff up here, mostly from the Fremont Indians, who were contemporaries of the Anasazi, who weren't quite this far north. The great-grandkids of some of the Swaseys just donated a huge collection to the museum up in Price."

Millie added, "There's some great Swasey stories, like the story of Swasey's Leap. There's a place right above the Black Box where the canyon narrows to about 20 feet, several hundred feet directly above the river. One of the Swasey boys dared the other to jump it on his horse, and he did. Stories like that. I think they all had a death wish —oh, geez, I shouldn't say that after Joe."

"Millie, were you and Joe good friends?" Bud asked.

"Yes, I would say so, as good as you can be with a hermit. Joe would come by the cafe about every day, and I'd give him a free lunch. It was just my way of being charitable, feeding him, just like the ravens. Sometimes I would get him stuff in town that he needed, but not really that often. He actually was a good-hearted guy. I think that was his problem, life was just too hard for him, so he retreated."

"Do you know anything about his past?" asked Roger.

"Not a lot. He was pretty secretive, didn't share much. All I know is he'd been divorced and worked the coal mines over by Huntington for awhile, then came up here. He had some kind of small military pension from some injury he'd got while in the Army, some war exercise in Nevada. That old cabin he was living in belonged to one of his early relatives up here. It's probably a hundred years old at the least. I bet there isn't one square inch of this country a Swasey hasn't set foot on."

They sat there in silence for awhile. Three ravens wheeled in the distance, above the yellow cliffs.

"I think he was killed because he knew something," Millie added, quietly. "I hope it's OK to talk about this, Bud." She glanced towards Roger.

"Millie, Roger's my right-hand man up here as of today. In fact, if anything comes up and Larry's not around, you can come to Roger."

"Well, that's good to know," Millie replied. "Especially since Larry's leaving tomorrow. He's got a long haul down into New Mexico."

"What's he hauling these days?" Bud asked.

"Dy-no-mite," Millie answered. "Dino-Noble Explosives. You couldn't pay me enough to haul something like that. He's a fool."

She stood. "You boys come on over and I'll make you some pizza for dinner."

"Thanks, Millie," Bud replied, "but I'm going to head on down the hill. My wife thinks I ran away from home. I've hardly even seen her since all this started."

"Oh, Bud, there is one thing I forgot to tell you about the last break-in. Well, two. Someone stole my wheelbarrow, and somebody left a note. All it said was, 'I'm sorry.'"

Bud shook his head. A vandal who leaves notes apologizing for his destruction? He'd never heard of such a thing.

"Did you keep it?" He asked.

"I did. It's locked in the cash register. Come on over to the cafe," Millie replied.

Just then, two geology students, a guy and a girl, came running over, excited.

"Sheriff Shumway," the girl said. "We just found a grave. It looks really fresh. I think you might want to come take a look."

14

Bud and Roger stood over what appeared to be a small grave, like maybe that of a child. It did indeed look fresh, dirt piled at its side, and Bud felt a little queasy at the thought of having to excavate it.

The two geology students, Carrie and Jim, stood there, silent. Finally, Jim asked, "Are you going to have to dig it up, Sheriff?"

Carrie added, "Maybe it's somebody's dog."

Jim answered, "Way up here? Who would come up here to bury their dog? And have to hike a half-mile from the nearest road to do it?"

Carrie replied, "Well, they might if it were a stolen dog or something. Or maybe it's a calf or something someone rustled. Hey, isn't that a petrified sponge?"

"Where?" Jim asked, excited.

Carrie pushed a little bit of dirt off the grave and pulled out what looked exactly like a small sponge, but hard as a rock.

Now she was excited, too. "It is! Cretaceous, dude!"

Roger looked at Bud. "There's a clue there, Sheriff," he pointed out.

Bud felt again like Howie must feel occasionally. He thought a bit, wishing again he had his sunglasses, then finally gave up, asking, "What?"

"The sponge. It's a marine fossil, obviously, but the grave is in the Curtis, which is eolian, or sand dunes. That means winds, not water."

Bud thought for a minute. "Good observation. It means the dirt was brought in. But why would someone bring in dirt for a grave? That's just crazy. You refill a grave with the dirt from the hole."

"That's true," Roger said. "And it looks like the dirt from the hole is in that pile over there. Looks like the grave has been moved from somewhere else. And look at these wheelbarrow tracks—whoever did it was the one who stole Millie's wheelbarrow."

Bud's head was starting to hurt. Why would someone move a grave up here? It was already in a spot that normally no one would have ever found. If the students hadn't been walking around all over, Bud was sure it would never have been discovered. But what was in it? There was only one way to find out, and he knew what that was.

He had grabbed Millie's shovel when they'd said they'd found a grave. Now it was time to use it.

Carrie and Jim suddenly decided they were probably missed and needed to get back to the cafe, so they took off on the hike back.

Bud delayed a bit by looking around for tracks, but they had inadvertently walked all over whatever might have been there. He went back to the grave, leaning on his shovel.

"What do you supposed is in there?" He asked Roger.

"Only one way to find out," Roger replied. "Look, Sheriff, give me the shovel. I'm the expert here."

"You are?" Bud asked. "How so?"

"I'm an archaeologist."

Roger started digging.

"You are?" Bud asked. "I thought you were a geology student."

"I'm that, too. My second degree is geology, as soon as this capstone class is over, in just a few more days. I want to go into geoarchaeology. But I've already done plenty of digs. I worked for the park service."

Roger was quickly getting things done. He paused for a moment, sifting the dirt through his fingers.

"Now we're getting into another type of soil. OK, just as I thought, it looks like limestone, buried under the native soil here, the Curtis. Whatever this is, the person just apparently dug it up, dirt and all, threw it into the wheelbarrow, and reburied it here."

Bud was impressed and said so. He then added that he had good insight into deputies, and he knew Roger was a good candidate the minute he met him. He thought of Howie, but decided not to say anything.

Now Roger stopped. He'd hit something. It was off-white, like bone. He was now tugging on it, pushing a little dirt away, then gently tugging again.

It occurred just then to Bud that if he were home, he and Hoppie could be enjoying more of that leftover meat loaf together, and that would be nice.

Now Roger was examining something. He handed it to Bud, who wasn't so sure he wanted it. He was a small-town sheriff, and murder wasn't his normal cup of tea—or coffee, in Bud's case. In fact, he suddenly pictured the Chow Down and wondered how everything was going down there.

"What is it?" He asked before holding out his hand.

"Well, it's a first for me, Sheriff," Roger replied. He handed it to Bud. "It's canvas. I think we just found the final resting place of Joe's paintings."

The paintings were now in shreds, what was left of them, and Bud took a few samples to take back to his office. The frames had been twisted and broken into small pieces. Bud noticed that Roger had put a small handful of dirt into his pocket.

Bud decided they should fix the grave back like it was, in case whoever had buried the paintings decided to come back. They did this, trying to brush all their footprints away, then hiked back to the cafe.

There, Bud ordered some coffee, then decided he should check in and see how things were going back at the office. He called Howie on his cell phone.

"Sheriff's office, Bud." Howie answered.

"Howie, it's Bud. How come you answer the phone like that?"

"Like what?"

Bud tried not to be impatient. "Why do you say Bud? I'm Bud."

"I know that, Sheriff. That's how *you* always answer it."

"But I'm Bud," he said. He was getting exasperated.

"I know you're Bud, even though I always call you Sheriff. I'm trying to get used to the idea of calling you that, that's all."

"How can you tell it's me calling?"

"Cause nobody else ever does. You comin' in today at all, Sheriff?" he asked.

"That's why I'm calling. It doesn't appear so."

"You still workin' at home?" Howie sounded envious, even though he hadn't done much all day in the office, unless you call reading magazines doing something.

"No, I'm up at the Ghost Rock. Anything going on down there?"

"Well," Howie answered, "I solved a burglary all by myself today. Other than that, not much."

Bud was surprised. "A burglary? What happened?"

"Old Man Green called in and someone had stolen two of his steers. They were missing, just like that, and the gate was closed and every-thing. So I went out there and looked around. We did a recount, and they were all there, but two were missing. It was kind of turning into a mystery. How could all the steers be there, and yet two be missing?"

"I have no idea, Howie, it's a riddle. You tell me."

"I finally asked him for more details, and he said the two missing ones had white on their faces. So I got up on the fence and looked pretty hard at those steers, and I found the two missing ones."

"How so, Howie?"

"They were covered with mud. Case solved. Green was pretty happy about that."

"Nice work, Howie," Bud said. He knew Old Man Green hit the

bottle every so often, and this must've been one of those every so oftens.

"I'll see you tomorrow, Howie."

"Roger," Howie said. "Oh, one other thing. I had a sub over at Howie's, you know, my old place, and I overheard a rumor."

"What's that?" Bud asked.

"They're talking about moving the sheriff's office over to Castle Dale, since that's where the courthouse is. Bud, I really don't like that town, as it's where my ex-wife lives. I might have to go back into the restaurant business to stay here."

"Howie, it's just a rumor, and it's not the first time it's made the rounds. I wouldn't worry about it too much. See you tomorrow."

15

Bud decided to call Wilma Jean and see how things were going. She was glad to hear from him and was wondering where he was. She was all excited, as she'd conjured up a bunch of new leagues for the bowling alley—Moonlight Bowling, Bowling for Dollars, that sort of thing.

She told him she had a surprise for him when he got home, and even though she wouldn't be there, the surprise would, and she knew he would really really like it. Bud kind of hoped it was country fried chicken and mashed potatoes with gravy.

He put his phone away and considered what he needed to do next. Millie was working in the kitchen, so he went back there.

"Millie, I'm sorry to intrude like this, but I need to ask you something, and I don't want the whole darn cafe to hear." A number of the geology students were in the cafe, along with a few tourists.

"Ask away," Millie said, flipping hamburgers with a spatula. "But you know it's illegal for you to be in here without having a food handler's license. But I guess the sheriff probably wouldn't arrest you this time, seeing how you're in on it with him."

Bud laughed, then said, "What did you mean earlier when you said you thought someone was trying to keep Joe quiet?"

"I dunno," Millie replied, shrugging. "I was just speculating. I really don't know why I think that, call it a hunch."

Bud continued, "Do you have anything at all to base it on?"

"Not really. It's just that when people are killed, there's either love or money involved. Joe wouldn't have had to worry about the love part, so it had something to do with money." She was now making gravy. It looked really good to Bud. He figured he must be hungry.

"How could Joe be involved with anything monetary up here? I mean, what's up here that could make anyone money?"

Millie looked at Bud and shook her head. "You're asking me, of all people?"

"OK," he replied. "But what does the Swell have that Joe could possibly turn into money?"

"Silver," she answered. "And I don't like the looks of the guy that geology prof's hanging out with. He drives a gray pickup, and he hangs with the prof on his days off. He's kind of smarmy. I think they're looking for something, and all I could imagine would be silver. There used to be a little silver around here. That would be my guess. Maybe Joe got on the wrong side of them somehow."

"Professor Cole?" Bud was surprised. "He doesn't look like he could kill a can of beer, yet alone a person."

"You never know what a person is capable of until you see them chasing after money," she replied, slapping a hamburger on a piece of Texas toast. "Or love. And don't underestimate that guy's drinking abilities. After all, he's a geologist. Here, you probably haven't eaten all day. On the house."

With that, she poured creamy gravy on the hamburger and handed the plate to Bud.

～

Bud sat in a booth, finishing what was left of his dinner, glad he hadn't waited to get home. Millie was right, he'd been hungry. Sleuthing around did that to one.

It was nearly dark, and he needed to go talk to Roger. He asked

Millie which room Roger was in and was going out the door when she said, "Don't forget this," and handed him the note from the cash register. He studied it for a moment before putting it into his jacket pocket. *I'm sorry* was almost a scribble.

Bud walked out the door and almost bumped into Professor Cole. He could see the tail lights of a gray pickup on the freeway ramp.

"Evening, Prof," Bud said cordially.

"Hello, Sheriff. How's everything going?"

"Oh, fine, I guess. Hey, got a minute? I want to ask you a couple of quick questions."

"Sure," the prof answered, leaning against the side of the building. The neon lights of the cafe lit up his glasses—red, white, yellow, red, white, yellow.

"I'll get right to the point. What were you and your friend, can't remember his name, doing in Swasey's cabin the other night?"

"I wasn't in the cabin."

"But your friend was."

"Jim Wilson. Yes, he did go inside. I told him not to. It had yellow tape around it, that's why I wouldn't go in."

"But you had planned to?"

"I was thinking about it, yes, but I didn't want to break the law when I saw the crime tape," the prof answered.

Bud figured he was being honest.

"Why go into the old cabin?" he asked.

"Sheriff, I would really like to tell you, but if I do, I'll be breaking the law."

"That's exactly what Jimmy said. How in the heck is it breaking the law to talk to the sheriff?"

"Look, I know this it probably a real puzzler for you, so I'll tell you. I would be breaking a confidentiality agreement. It's contractual, in writing, and an attorney was involved in creating it, so I really don't want to break it. Talking to you would violate the contract."

"Professor, such agreements are invalid when a law officer is questioning you, you know that."

"I don't know that, Sheriff. And until I do for a fact, I can't say anything more. Actually, I will say one more thing, but in the form of a question. You told me you would be at the cabin, so why weren't you?"

"I was," Bud answered.

"I didn't see hide nor hair of you. If you'd been there like you said you would, Jim wouldn't have needed to go into the cabin."

"Why not?" Bud asked.

"Because you could have instead. I can't say any more, but you can rest assured that neither of us had anything to do with Joe's death. I heard he died from a wild animal attack, but if someone killed him, it had nothing to do with us. I'll contact the attorney and get back with you, Sheriff, but it may take awhile. In the meantime, go home and get some rest. You look pretty haggard."

Bud didn't like hearing that, but he knew it was probably true. But he figured he wouldn't be having any more bad dreams, now that he knew the Bigfoot was a hoax, so maybe tonight he'd get some sleep.

But first, he had to talk to Roger. He knocked on his motel room door.

"Come in," Roger's voice boomed out. The door was unlocked, so Bud stepped inside. Roger was reading a book, something about the geologic history of the Colorado Plateau.

"Sheriff!" he looked surprised. "You're still up here? You need to go home. You look really tired."

"So I've been told," Bud answered. "Roger, take a good look at this note. I'm taking it back for evidence, but see if you can get over to Swasey's cabin tomorrow and find a sample of his handwriting."

Roger was surprised. "Swasey? Why would he break into the cafe? He and Millie were friends."

"I know," answered Bud, "And why else would someone write an apology note, unless they cared?"

"Good point," Roger said. "But the timing is all off. Wouldn't Joe have been dead by the time of the second break in?"

"Yes, but someone could've taken a note he'd already written for some other reason and planted it. I know it sounds crazy, but I have to consider every possible angle and be thorough."

"OK, I'll go over there tomorrow. Now go get some rest."

"Roger, and 10-4 Roger," Bud kidded. "You know, I've always wanted to work with someone named Roger so I could say that. Anyway, I'm outta here, but be really careful around that cabin. I have a suspicion that whoever is involved in this still has something going on there, if nothing else, that darn Bigfoot costume. They're sure to come and get it at some point. I don't want you to compromise your safety for any reason, agreed?"

"Roger, I'm agreed," Roger agreed.

16

Bud pulled into his drive. Wilma Jean was gone, and the porch light was off. Not good. Maybe she'd just forgot to turn it on and wasn't mad at him, he hoped, although it sure didn't make for finding his way to the house very easy.

Careful as he was in the pitch dark, he still managed to catch his toe on the edge of the flower bed. He almost went down, but grabbed the door handle just in time.

Now Hoppie was barking madly, having heard him. But something was different about his voice, and he sounded a bit like he'd caught a cold.

Bud hoped he was OK. Maybe it had been a bit too chilly to leave him in the yard yesterday, although he'd seemed fine when he got back. He needed to get busy and put in a dog door so Hoppie could go in and out when he wanted. Maybe he would need it himself, if Wilma Jean ever got really mad at him.

Bud opened the door, but before he could reach around to turn on the light, he felt something attack, almost knocking him off his feet. Hoppie was there, still barking madly, but something was wrong.

Now whatever had attacked him was chewing on his ankle, growling, and Hoppie was jumping up on Bud, happy to see him, almost knocking him over.

Bud managed to push whatever was chewing on him away and flip on the light. Standing at his feet, growling, was a black-and-tan wiener dog. Bud remembered Wilma Jean telling him she had a surprise, and now he deduced it wasn't a hot dinner, but an insane little dachshund instead. He flashed on a picture he'd seen once of a wiener dog all dressed up in a bun.

So, Wilma Jean had gotten another dog, Bud surmised, trying to get the little dog to come to him. It was barking like it had just cornered a burglar, but the more Bud talked to it, the more it calmed down and even started wagging its tail. Bud was finally able to pick it up and pet it. He wondered if it, too, would sleep at Wilma Jean's feet. They would have to get another little bed to add on to the bottom of theirs.

Wilma Jean had already gotten tags for it. Bud pulled the dog's collar around where he could read them. They said, "Peer."

Great, Bud thought, a wiener dog that's not house trained. He thought about it, thinking that was a strange name for a dog. Then he decided that maybe it referred to the dog's status in the household, as all their previous dogs had pretty much been their peers—in fact, some of them had actually ranked above them, as it seemed like they ran the household.

Bud looked at the tag again. "Pierre." That made more sense, a wiener dog named Pierre. A dog of German heritage with a French name, two countries that had traditionally disliked each other. This little guy's in for some cognitive dissonance, he surmised, putting the dog down, where it immediately began chewing on his pant leg again.

Bud hobbled into the kitchen, where he saw a note from Wilma Jean on the counter.

Hon, dinner in the oven, give the dogs some. Doctor Richardson called and wants you to call him if you get in before too late. XXXOOO

Bud looked at the clock on the kitchen wall, the dog with the big eyes and clock on its tummy with a tail that moved as the clock ticked. It was only seven o'clock. He had plenty of time to call the doc, and he would call him now, no use thinking about it while he was eating dinner. He wanted to relax.

Bud dialed the number and sat down in his big lounger in the living room, Pierre still attached to his pant leg, dragging along.

"Hello, Bud, how's everything going?" Doc Richardson answered. Bud hated caller ID, as it took all the surprise out of everything.

"Good, Doc, and you?"

"Fine, fine. We're sure having some beautiful spring weather up this way. How about down in Green River?"

"Same. The globe willows are all greening up."

"No kidding? They're not here, but you guys are lower and always ahead of us. How's the investigation going?"

This surprised Bud, as he thought he'd made it clear to Doc that he agreed it was an animal attack.

"Fine. I've been up at the cafe talking to Millie so I can write up a report for her insurance." He hoped he'd dodged that bullet.

"Did they do a lot of damage?"

"Some, but not too bad. She's hoping to get her windows paid for, if nothing else."

"Good, I hope she does. That was a shame. Any idea who did it?"

"No, I think it may have just been someone coming through on the freeway looking for an easy way to get some cash." Bud answered.

"Did they take any money?"

"No. Millie got lucky there."

"Did they take anything else?"

Bud was beginning to wonder why Doc was so interested.

"They stole a couple of paintings, but other than that, no."

It was as if the doc had read his mind, because he said, "I have an interest in this, Bud. I know Millie's having a hard time up there, and she's fed me many a delicious meal when I was on my way through. I'd like to give her a little anonymous donation to help out. Would you mind delivering it?"

"Not at all, Doc. That's very generous of you, and I know she'll really appreciate it."

"I can afford it. Things are going well for me. My youngest daughter just finished med school and that won't be on my budget any more."

"Congrats, Doc, that's really something to be proud of. Where will she practice?"

"She's wanting to stay over in Colorado, probably in Grand Junction. But Bud, there's something else..."

"What's that, Doc?" Bud asked, feeling a bit wary again.

"I heard you guys really need a new vehicle down there. One of my friends is a Shriner, and he told me about what's going on. I'd like to add five grand to the pool. I'll send two checks in the mail, one for the car and one for Millie. I'm giving her five grand, also. If you don't mind, please cash it and give it to her anonymously."

"I don't mind a bit," Bud replied.

Pierre was now chewing up his pant leg, but he was too shocked to even notice as he hung up the phone, thinking about that Toyota Land Cruiser and what color would be best. Maybe a forest green, if they made them, the color of all the money that seemed to be flowing his way.

He went back into the kitchen and opened the oven. Baked chicken, and on the stove was a pan with mashed potatoes and another with gravy. It was time to buy Wilma Jean some flowers, Bud thought, while making himself, Hoppie, and now little Pierre each a plate.

17

The next day, Bud had dropped the gorilla suit hair sample into the mail and was finishing his report on the Ghost Rock Cafe break-ins when he got a call.

"Sheriff's office, Bud."

"Sheriff, I need some advice."

"Is that you, Howie? What's up?"

He'd sent the deputy out to do traffic control on an old historic farm house that was being moved into town, not that there was much traffic to control.

"They can't seem to get this darn house across the bridge here at the river."

"The highway bridge across the Green? What's the problem, it's a two-lane bridge, should be plenty of room."

"Well, there should be, but they're having problems."

Bud tried not to be annoyed. Sometimes he felt like a fry cook, having to grill Howie for everything.

"What kind of problems, Howie?"

"The house kind of slipped off the truck, and it's blocking the bridge. Traffic's starting to back up. I don't know what to do."

"Kind of slipped off the truck? OK, Howie, I'll be right out."

Bud got into his old Bronco, thinking about the license plate check he had just done on Jimmy Wilson's truck. The truck wasn't registered to Jimmy Wilson at all, but to a second party, Mancos Resources, Inc. in Price.

Bud was surprised, but now he thought he had more of an inkling of what might be going on. He wasn't sure what Mancos Resources did, but a company named after the Mancos shales of the Green River region had to be a mineral exploration company of some sort.

He pulled up to the end of the bridge, where Howie waited in the cruiser, his lights flashing. He looked upset, Bud thought, and his face was red. Not a good sign. You had to be patient in this business, and also a bit thick skinned.

Right smack in the middle of the bridge, blocking both lanes, sat a big two-story farm house, tipped precariously where it had half-slipped off the big beams carrying it behind a truck. Two guys stood there, looking helpless, as traffic began to back up.

"Howie," Bud said. "Go on out the west exit onto the freeway, then come back around to the east exit and set up a road block until they get this figured out. I'll stay here and see what I can do."

Howie looked relieved, got into the old cruiser, and headed west.

Bud left his Bronco right in the middle of the road, lights flashing, and walked onto the bridge to where the two fellows were talking. They had called a crane in Grand Junction. Bud figured the house movers had just lost their profit and then some.

The two fellows, resigned to a long wait, walked across the bridge and into the nearby truck stop, the Eastwinds, which was on the east end of town, appropriately enough. Another, called the Westwinds, set on the west end, and the two had a bitter rivalry going for what little business the town managed to have.

There wasn't much the house movers could do until the crane arrived. Bud felt they were being pretty nonchalant, but if the house tipped any further, maybe they didn't want to witness its demise, along with that of their house-moving business, which he suspected was also about to crash anyway.

He now walked on across the bridge, stopping to examine the

house a bit, fiddling with his sunglasses. It looked like it could tip any second into the river. Someone should start a betting pool on when.

Gawkers were already coming onto the bridge, taking photos and talking excitedly. This was a big event for Green River, and word was quickly getting out. It was big enough for a town reporter to cover, if they only had one.

Bud talked a bit to a few of the drivers waiting on the east side of the bridge while directing traffic back around. They would have to go back onto the freeway and take the other exit to access the town. He could see Howie's lights flashing back up the road.

He then decided he'd better stay there to keep anyone from walking onto the bridge. It could be a potentially dangerous situation. He needed a third deputy, someone to guard the other end of the bridge.

It was then he spied Wilma Jean's big pink Lincoln. She had found out what was going on, and, as the town's pulse, she needed to investigate. Sometimes Bud thought she would make a better sheriff than he did, or maybe a news reporter. He noticed two little heads sticking out of the car window. Must be Hoppie and Pierre.

He called her on his cell phone.

"Hi, Hon, what's going on?" she answered.

"Not much more than what you see. There's a crane on its way from Junction, but it's gonna take awhile. Look, can you stay over on that end of the bridge and keep people from coming on until I can get ahold of someone else to help out?" he asked.

"Sure," she replied. "I can stay here for as long as you need me. Isn't Pierre a cutie?"

Bud conceded he was, and he could now see her big Lincoln pull over next to his Bronco. She got out and sat on its hood, and soon had a group of people around her.

Wilma Jean was kind of the opposite of Bud in some ways. She was a lot more gregarious and had lots of friends. They would probably have a wine and cheese party going over there before long, Bud noted.

Now a white Ford pickup had pulled right up to his side of the bridge, and someone Bud knew from long ago got out. It was Henry Tidwell of the hay theft caper, Jimmy Wilson's cousin.

They exchanged pleasantries, talked a bit about the house, speculated on its possible collapse, then got down to business.

Henry asked, "Say, Sheriff, my cousin Jimmy said you'd met him at the cafe downtown and was wondering about a few things. Seems like you were interrogating him. What the heck's going on?"

Bud was now on guard, and even though Henry helped pay his salary with his taxes, he knew well enough that he wasn't obligated to share anything with him on the information front.

Bud said, "See that good-lookin' gal over there by that pink car? That's my wife. She can fill you in on all the Green River news, it's not part of my job." He was miffed and didn't try to hide it.

Henry started backpedaling so hard Bud thought he might run into the river.

"No, no, that's not what I meant. I know you're doing an investigation about poor old Joe Swasey, and I just wanted to add some information. You know, Bud, I kind of owe you one. That hay business was a bad deal. I temporarily lost my senses, was just laid off and was worried about how I was gonna feed my cattle. You kept me out of jail, and I know it. I don't know if I ever even thanked you, but I am now."

Bud softened a bit, but was still wary. He knew every trick in the book because it had been used on him, and he knew when he was being buttered up.

"That's OK. What's up, Henry. What do you need to tell me?"

"I want to tell you this. Jimmy's kind of a hard character in some ways, as it seems to run on that side of the family, but he didn't kill Joe. I guess I feel a bit defensive of him. He's had a hard go of things."

"How do you know Joe was killed by a human? Seems like the consensus right now is an animal did it." Bud was getting suspicious.

"Look, Bud, I can tell you this, my cousin has an alibi. He was at my house when the murder or whatever it was happened."

Bud was wondering if he had a case for arresting Henry for

obstructing justice or something. Instead, he replied, "How do you know exactly when Joe was killed?"

Henry didn't blink an eye. "I know exactly when it happened because I was nearby. It was Saturday, mid-afternoon. I was out looking for some strays on horseback, not far from Joe's cabin. I heard Joe yelling, then I heard what sounded like a shotgun, and then I heard him calling out for help. He was yelling, "Help, Help," and he sounded like a dying man to me."

Henry paused, then continued. "By the time I got there, maybe five minutes at the most, there was nobody around, nary a soul. There were two young guys not too far away, maybe a half mile, but I don't think they had anything to do with it. Looked like they were out surveying or something. But Jimmy was down at my place in town at a family reunion, and about 40 people can testify to that."

"Why didn't you come to me about what you heard?" Bud asked, still suspicious.

"I didn't know for sure that anything had happened. Like I said, I went over to the cabin, but I didn't see anything or anybody. Besides, I can't say I have the best of associations with your office, no offense."

"Did you go inside the cabin?" Bud asked.

"I looked in there, but it was empty. But you know, Bud, if someone murdered Joe, it wouldn't surprise me one bit."

"Why not?"

"He was a thief. He rustled cattle. That's how he stayed alive up there. He stole calves and butchered them."

"Do you have proof of this?"

"I've had at least a half-dozen calves go missing, and Bert Miles, he's lost some, too."

Bud was now wondering if maybe he didn't have a new suspect, but it seemed odd that Henry would have come to him if he'd been the murderer.

Bud asked, "How do you know they weren't killed by cougars or something else?"

"Because cougars will typically drag their kill away, then eat on them for days. And there aren't many cougars left up there. They don't eat part of them and then just abandon their kill."

"But how do you know it was Joe killing the calves?"

"Because of the way they were butchered. Not to get graphic, Sheriff, but humans are the only ones capable, it would take hands. And Joe's the only human up there, except Millie. And Joe probably learned a lot from his relatives. There were rumors they had done a little rustling over the years."

"That doesn't prove Joe did it. It could be anyone. Maybe even a Bigfoot," Bud added, watching Henry's eyes. He was about to ask Henry what Jimmy was looking for up on the Swell, but thought better of it, remembering Professor Cole's confidentiality agreement. There might be things he'd like to know, but he wasn't going to jeopardize the professor.

Henry studied Bud for a moment, then added, "I didn't rule that one out, either. I've seen some strange things up there myself. In fact, I thought I saw a Bigfoot once up there, not far from Swasey's cabin, but that was years ago."

Now Henry changed the subject. "By the way, I think you need a raise so you can get yourself some decent clothes." He pointed to Bud's pant leg, which was almost chewed into two parts, right at the ankle.

About then, people started yelling, and a huge splash diverted their attention as the old farm house tipped into the river, slowly sinking part way into the currents, headed on a new adventure downstream to the confluence with the Colorado River and then on down to Glen Canyon Dam.

Bud groaned, then got on the phone to the Bureau of Reclamation and Canyonlands National Park on downstream.

18

Bud and Wilma Jean sat on a retaining wall next to the River Museum, talking about the events of the past week. They both had the day off together, a rare event. Hoppie and Pierre played on the big grassy lawn, ignoring the "No Dogs" sign.

They had all been on a nice long walk, first coming up Long Street from the house, then across town, and now they were resting in front of the museum, watching the river. The plan was to go across the street to the Willows Restaurant, tie the dogs outside and have lunch, then walk back home.

Bud's cell phone rang, and he now worried that their plan would soon be thwarted. He didn't want to answer, but the caller ID indicated it could be Roger, so he decided he'd better.

"Bud here."

"Sheriff, it's me, Roger."

"I thought that might be you, with that Salt Lake prefix," Bud said. "Isn't the School of Mines in Salt Lake?"

Bud was feeling a bit detached. He didn't want to think about anything. It was his day off, and he was still tired.

"Sheriff, yes, good news. I found the grave."

"What grave?" Bud asked.

"The original grave, the one that was dug up and reburied."

"What?"

"You know, the grave with Joe's paintings in it. It looks like they were originally buried over by the cabin. I found the hole, and the dirt matches perfectly. Like I thought, Carmel Formation."

"Good work, Rog," Bud said. "Now what in the heck does it mean? Why rebury something?"

Roger answered, "I think it means whoever did it was getting nervous and worrying about them being found over by the cabin, so they moved them."

"Probably. Good thinking." Bud just wasn't on it today. Wilma Jean was giving him that impatient look again. She was ready to go eat.

Roger continued, "And I went through everything at the cabin, I mean everything. I got several samples of Joe's writing, and Bud, I don't think he wrote that note. The writing's different."

"Good work," Bud said, then added, "But why did anyone care about Joe's paintings?"

"I can't answer that yet, but I'm working on it," Roger answered.

Bud felt a bit ashamed of himself. He needed to get a grip. This young guy had nothing to gain by solving this crime, and yet he was fully engaged, and Bud was acting like he expected him to come up with the answers. It made Bud feel like a slacker. But he was tired.

"I also went over to the alcove, and everything's gone, the Bigfoot suit, everything."

"No kidding?"

"And get this, guess what else I got? I hope you don't mind me taking it."

"What?"

"Joe's rock collection. He had a huge rock collection. It was in a little lean-to over behind the cabin, all hidden with overgrown rabbit brush. I got everything, Sheriff, and it's awesome. There were even two Fremont pots, and they're beauts."

He paused, then added, "Millie went over with me. I hope that's OK, but no way could I carry that stuff. We got her old caddie in there. It took three loads in her trunk. I'm hiding everything in my room until you can get up here, but I'm hoping you won't take it all for evidence, 'cause there are rocks there like I've never seen before and I'd like to keep."

Only a geologist would haul three loads of rocks to his motel room, Bud thought.

"Roger, don't say a word about any of this to anyone, not even Professor Cole—especially not Professor Cole, understand? And warn Millie, too. And hide those pots somewhere in your room where no one but you could find them. They may be illegal."

"Millie says they look like the ones Joe painted for her. I mean, exactly. He used them as models. But are you suspecting the prof had something to do with Joe's murder? Or is it in my place to ask? After all, I am a deputy." Roger sounded a bit put off, like he wasn't in the inner circle any more or something.

"No, Rog, it's not like that. Look, you know Professor Cole is a consultant, and they're looking for something. And that something might just be involved with that collection. I'm just speculating, but let's just keep a lid on everything for now, because it could be that it's connected to the murder somehow."

"I see what you mean," Roger replied. "OK, I'm going over to the cafe to talk to Millie, so I'm gonna go."

"Roger, Roger," Bud said. "Nice work, and be careful."

∽

Lunch at the Willows was a treat that Bud and Wilma Jean usually saved for special occasions, but today they just felt like eating out. Maybe the special occasion was seeing each other for once.

They were enjoying the view of the Green River through the huge plate glass windows when Bud's phone rang. It was Professor Krider, and Bud felt obligated to take the call, seeing what the prof had done for him in the new vehicle department.

"Bud here."

"Hello, Bud. Krider here. I hope I'm not interrupting anything, as I know it's your day off."

"Wilma Jean and I are having lunch, but it's OK." She shot him a look that told him it wasn't OK.

"Bud, I'm wondering if I could get you to come over for a bit this afternoon, and for once, it doesn't have anything to do with a book I'm working on. Wilma Jean's welcome to come, too. I'm thinking of buying a melon farm down by the river, and I'd like to get your input on it. You know I really respect your common sense. We have permission to go out there, and I thought maybe you'd come down and walk around a bit with me to check it out."

"You know, Prof, that sounds absolutely great. I need something like that as a break. How about in a couple of hours?"

"See you then."

B ud and Professor Krider were walking down the edge of a freshly plowed field. It was almost time to plant, and the melon farmer who owned the farm was riding a big tractor, carefully preparing the soil. Huge cottonwood trees grew along a big irrigation ditch that fed from a diversion dam down at the river.

Green River melons were famous, and the farmers of the area took great pride in raising the sweetest and juiciest. Melons seemed to love the desert climate, the hot days and cool nights. The temperature fluctuation is what made them store sugar, and they also liked the sandy soil.

"This is a beautiful place, Prof," Bud stated the obvious. "I would love to have a place like this. How many acres?"

"Almost 200," Krider replied. "Big enough to keep a man really busy, yet small enough to be manageable—with help, of course. You need a lot of acreage to grow melons, because you have to rotate the crops. After a couple of years, you need to grow something else in the soil for awhile, so it takes a couple of hundred acres to grow about 50 acres of melons. I want to start growing seedless melons. Even though it costs more, the demand is higher."

"Would you stop writing mysteries?"

"No, I'd still write. It's a curse, being a writer. It's kind of like I picture being an alcoholic, hard to quit. But melon farming would feed another need I've had since I was a kid. I grew up on a farm and have always wanted to go back."

"Me, too," Bud said, a bit jealous. He wished he were a farmer right now. It sounded like paradise.

The prof replied, "I'm a little surprised. I thought you enjoyed law enforcement."

"I usually do, but to tell you the truth, Prof, right now I'm pretty burned out. This Swasey murder really has me wound up, and I can't figure anything much out."

"Maybe I can help, if you want to share the details."

"Prof, I can't discuss police matters with anyone but another officer, you know that, but I truly am at my wit's end."

"Well," the prof answered, "Why don't you just deputize me, then we can discuss it?"

Bud laughed. "Not a bad idea." He trusted the prof and knew he had a sharp sense for mysteries. He'd written at least ten so far, and they all had intricate plots that amazed Bud.

They sat down on an old melon shipping crate. Bud ended up telling the prof the details of his investigation, and when he was done, the prof just sat there, thinking.

He finally said, "Bud, I think you have an idea what's going on with Joe, but you're not wanting to see it."

Bud was surprised. He didn't think he had any idea at all as to what was going on.

"Right now, Prof, it could be anyone. Even a wild animal. The body was so messed up it's hard to tell. I'm suspecting about everyone up there: Professor Cole, Henry Tidwell, his cousin Jimmy, and heck, even Millie, though no way could I picture her doing it. And the doc."

"All I can say is this, Bud, whoever buried those paintings and then freaked out and came back, dug them up, then moved them, is scared to death they'll be caught. This isn't the work of a true criminal, a seasoned sociopath with no conscience. Rather, it's the work of someone who probably didn't really understand the consequences of what they were doing until after they committed the murder. My advice is to look for the person who has the most to lose. In my experience, they're the ones who are the most scared."

Bud sat and thought about that. It made sense, but he wasn't sure who that would be.

They stood to go, and the prof added, "I think I'm going to buy this farm. And you know, Bud, you can always come to work here, anytime you want. That's a standing offer, so don't let the detective work get you down. You're up to the task, but if you decide to quit, come over here. I would really enjoy having someone of your caliber manage this place for me. I would match what you're making now, or even more."

As Bud drove away, he felt a huge sense of relief. He no longer felt stuck in his job. He could always work for Krider. He would go home and tell Wilma Jean and see what she thought of it, but he knew she'd say whatever he wanted to do was A-OK with her. She was like that.

He drove on home, enjoying the sunset for the first time in ages, ready to kick back and relish the evening with his family, all four of them snuggled together.

19

Bud slept well and woke up refreshed for the first time since he'd gotten the word that Joe Swasey had been killed.

As usual, Wilma Jean had gone to the cafe, but he made the kids, Hoppie and Pierre, a breakfast of bacon and eggs, enjoying a bit himself. He then decided to go for a drive before heading to the office.

He drove on down Long Street, the opposite direction of town, where Krider's future melon farm was. He wondered when Krider would buy it. The way he talked, soon.

Bud pulled over by the road for a moment and saw the farmer out in the field on his big tractor. He tried to picture what it would be like to sit on a tractor all day and just daydream instead of trying to solve other people's problems—problems they'd usually created themselves, and unnecessarily at that.

He sat there as long as he could, delaying going to the office. In fact, he dreaded going in, something that was a first for him. He truly was burned out, and he felt that Joe's murder was seriously trying his analytic abilities. Maybe he should just go along with the wild animal theory and forget the whole thing.

But that wasn't like him, and he knew it. He owed it to Joe to figure this out, and he also owed it to society as a whole, because if someone will kill once, they might do it again, given the right circumstances. That's why people went to prison, to protect other people—supposedly, anyway.

Bud finally turned his old Bronco around and headed to the office. He'd check into new vehicles, he thought, using that as an incentive to get back to work. He needed to call the Toyota dealer over in Grand Junction and see what Land Cruisers cost, even though he was having second thoughts about buying a vehicle that no one local could probably repair.

Bud parked next to Howie's cruiser, wondering how he was doing, as he hadn't heard a word from him since the house-moving incident the other day. That would normally mean things were quiet, but who knows? Maybe Howie had taken the helm and decided to fight crime all on his lonesome, since he was beginning to act like he thought Bud was a slacker. Maybe Howie was right.

"Morning, Sheriff," Howie said, turning from his desk and handing Bud an envelope. "Looks like something from the crime lab up in Salt Lake City."

Bud slowly opened it. He wasn't sure he wanted to know the results. Either way, whether it were definitive evidence or not, it would mean thinking about Joe's murder.

He sat reading the report while Howie waited to hear the news.

Finally, Howie could stand it no more and asked, "Is that the hamburger test you sent in, Sheriff?"

"It is," Bud answered. He slowly took the report and put it back into the envelope.

"Does it say anything?" Howie asked again.

"It does," Bud answered, kind of enjoying playing Howie's "you have to grill me for it" game back on him.

"Well, for cryin' out loud, Sheriff, what does it say?"

Bud replied, "It says they weren't able to find any fingerprints."

"Oh," Howie replied, totally deflated. "That's too bad. I was hoping it had something that would solve the crime."

"Me, too."

"Maybe it really was a wild animal attack," Howie offered.

"Yeah, maybe it was, Howie. I think I need to get back up there again, though, and talk to one last person before I close the case."

"Who would that be?"

"The guy who found Joe. A geology student named Todd."

"Didn't you already question him?"

"I did, but I forgot to ask one thing. In the meantime, call over to Grand Junction and see what the Toyota dealer wants for a Land Cruiser, new or used. I'll be back later this afternoon. Cover for me, Howie."

"I always do," Howie said, wondering if he could get away with bringing a small TV into the office.

He wouldn't mind watching old reruns of *Murder, She Wrote* or *Sherlock Holmes*, along with a few of his other favorites. Maybe he could write it off as an educational cost.

Bud was soon out the door, the envelope with the test in his jacket pocket. He felt kind of bad, not squaring with Howie about the hamburger test, but he wasn't sure he wanted anyone else to know, and he also wasn't so sure Howie could keep something like that to himself. What he'd told him was true, he just hadn't told him the whole truth.

He pulled himself into the old Bronco, put on his sunglasses, checked that his gun was in its holster, and tipped his cowboy hat back a bit.

The lab had been able to isolate a good DNA sample from some saliva on the hamburger, but it didn't match anyone's DNA that they had on file. If Bud could get a DNA sample from whoever he thought had been eating that hamburger or had possibly planted it, they could verify if it were them. It wasn't much, he thought, and he had no idea what something like that could prove, other than the person was there in the cabin at the time or after Joe's death.

Bud was now pushing his sunglasses up onto the bridge of his nose, thinking.

He was recalling what Henry had said about hearing Joe yelling. Henry's exact words were that he'd heard Joe calling out, "Help, Help." Maybe Henry was lying about the whole thing, but maybe not.

Whoever it had been, they hadn't planned on someone being around to hear when they killed Joe by whatever method they had used.

And if Joe had died a couple of days before his body was found, they had returned to the crime scene with the hamburger later, maybe the same time they'd moved the paintings.

Krider was right, they hadn't really planned it all out very well.

But murderers typically need a motive. What motive would anyone have for killing an old harmless hermit out on the Swell? Bud thought again of Joe's newfound artistic abilities. He knew there was a connection there, somehow.

Bud put the Bronco in reverse, where it stuck for a moment, backed around, then put it in first and headed back up the Swell, his sunglasses starting their journey back down the bridge of his nose, but this time he didn't even notice.

20

Larry was sitting in a booth opposite Millie when Bud walked into the Ghost Rock Cafe. He had on a ball cap with the words *Property of Dino-Noble Explosives* embroidered on it. Bud wasn't sure if it referred to the hat or to Larry.

"Millie," Larry was saying, "I bet this place was something else before the freeway ruined everything. I bet you had some interesting characters come through—cowboys, California hippies, old prospectors, all kinds of people—before it was all ruined."

Millie replied, "Yup, it was something else, for sure, 'cause it didn't exist before the freeway came through. There wasn't a highway here, Larry."

Larry looked surprised. "Then why the heck does it look so old and dilapidated? The freeway hasn't been here that long."

"Maybe it's because someone we both know isn't keeping up on their part of a deal," Millie answered, referring to their trading rent for work agreement.

Bud sat down next to Larry. He wanted to be able to see Millie's face.

"How's work going, Bud?" Larry asked.

"Fine. I'm about to declare the Swasey case closed. I think he was probably killed by an animal, after looking into things more closely." Bud saw Millie flinch.

"You sure about that, Sheriff?" She asked. He thought she seemed suddenly distant.

"Not one-hundred percent, but pretty much sure," he answered.

"Well, I gotta get back to work." She seemed irritated, and stood to leave.

Bud was now pretty sure Millie hadn't killed Joe. If she had, she would've been happy that he was closing the case, not miffed. But who knows, maybe she was a good actress.

"It's OK, Millie, sit back down."

She sat back down, looking puzzled.

"Millie, are you sure about not having seen Joe for a couple of days? Are you sure he didn't come over and get a burger?"

"I thought you just said you were sure Joe had been killed by an animal." She paused. "As for him not coming in, I would stake my life on it. I was worried about him. I was about ready to go over to his place myself and check on him when Todd found him instead.

"Millie, that hamburger was fresh. I'm thinking maybe it was planted, but I can't figure out why. At first I thought it might be poisoned, but that wasn't the case. And if Joe hadn't been over here for two days and was already dead, he couldn't have eaten it."

Bud paused, then asked, "Do you recall anyone else buying a take-out hamburger the day Joe was found?"

"Everyone did, the whole crew of geology students, except one girl, who's a vegetarian. They all had take-out burgers for lunch. It could've come from any one of them."

"What about Professor Cole?"

"He had a hamburger, too. Everyone did, except the one girl."

"How about some tourists, or anyone you know who just stopped by?"

"No, most people are ready for a break and want to eat here."

Larry interrupted, "I did. You forgot me, Millie. I ordered a hamburger to go, remember?"

"Did you kill Joe?" Bud asked, only half-kidding. At this point, he was beginning to suspect anyone and everyone.

"If I had, it would've been justified, but no, I didn't." Larry said. "I hope you're kidding, Bud."

"I had to ask, Larry, since you're the one who provided the possible clue. But why would it be justified?"

"Because Joe deserved it." Larry sounded angry, like someone with a long-standing grudge.

Millie protested, "Larry, you have to forget things. Joe was sorry, you know that. If I can forgive him, why can't you?"

"How did he deserve it?" Bud asked. He and Larry went way back —back clear to before Bud had moved to Green River, when they'd worked together in the uranium mines. Larry could never kill anyone, even if he was mad, Bud was sure of that.

"I don't want to talk about it. I'm sorry I brought it up," Larry said. "It's not important and had nothing to do with his death."

Bud sat there for a moment, hoping someone would say something. The silence was getting more and more uncomfortable.

Finally, he said, "Millie, I faxed the insurance report to your adjuster. Has he been up here yet?"

"Yes, he says he thinks they'll pay for the windows and maybe some of the other damage. I sure need the money. My taxes are due."

They all continued to sit there, no one saying anything more. Bud decided the discussion must be over and asked, "Do you know if Todd's around?"

Millie answered, "I saw him over at the motel not long ago."

Bud figured he should get up and go over there. If nobody wanted to tell him anything, there wasn't much he could do about it.

He put on his sunglasses and stood to go, when Larry finally offered, "Joe was killing Millie's ravens. He had no cause to do that, and we both told him to stop, but he kept on. Every day, we'd find another dead raven. It was torturing Millie, and I can't say I found it very palatable either."

Bud sat back down. "Why would he do something like that?"

"He said they were leading bad things to him, and he was afraid one day he'd get killed. You know, ravens will follow something and alert a predator to it so they can share the kill. Joe had a shotgun, and he was pretty damn good with it."

Bud thought of what Henry had said about hearing a shotgun. He then flashed on Doc Richardson's bruised hand.

"What kind of bad things were they supposedly leading to him?" he asked.

"Bigfoot," Larry replied.

Bud let out a deep breath. He couldn't believe what he was hearing—he needed to get some fresh air. He stood to go, and it was then that he remembered the money in his pocket.

"Millie, an anonymous donor sent this to you via my office. It's to help you get going again. Don't ask, 'cause I can't tell."

With that, he plunked a bank envelope containing $5,000 in one-hundred-dollar bills onto the table, turned, and walked away. He heard Millie gasp as he walked out the door.

21

Bud knocked on Roger's door, but no one answered. He had wanted to check in, see if Roger had found anything else and take a look at his new rock collection—and those Fremont pots, which he hoped were well-hidden. Roger must be out in the field.

He then knocked on Todd's door. Todd opened it, surprised to see Bud.

"Hey, Todd. How's everything going?" Bud asked, taking off his sunglasses in the dark room. Todd was watching *Kangaroo Express*, a kid's afternoon show. "Hope I'm not interrupting anything."

Todd turned off the TV.

"Nope," he said. "Just procrastinating my geology stuff."

"How's that all going, anyway?"

"OK. I'm kind of sick of it, to tell you the truth. I'm taking the rest of the day off, as I've finished my map for today."

"Todd, I'd like to ask you a few questions, if you don't mind."

Todd looked a bit nervous, but consented.

Bud continued, "I'd like to know more about your Bigfoot experience. You said you'd seen one that day you found Joe's body. Do you mind talking about it?"

"It wasn't that same day that I found Joe's body that I saw it," Todd replied.

"No, I meant that's when you told me that. Exactly when did you see it?"

"It was awhile before that. We'd all been camping out—I don't know if you're aware of it, but the original field camp was supposed to be exactly that, a field camp. But we kept seeing and hearing things, so we finally told Professor Cole if we couldn't go to the motel, we wanted to leave. He kinda sorta thought we were just making it all up so we wouldn't have to camp out, 'cause it's still cold up here at night, but then he heard it, too. That's when we came over here and rented out all the rooms."

"Where were you guys camped?"

"Over on the edge of Eagle Canyon. Not real far from Swasey's cabin. I can show you on my topo here."

He pulled out a map and pointed to the location. "You get in there off this little back road over here," he said, pointing to a small road on the map. It's actually more of an ATV trail. We had several ATVs, but our lab assistant took everything back to the school when she left, since she was driving the pickup with the ATV trailer. We also had some nice Springbar tents."

Bud studied the map for a bit, then asked, "What exactly did you see?"

Todd was quiet for awhile. "I kind of hate to remember it," he said. "It's made me afraid to be out there, and I don't like that. I used to really like hiking around and being outdoors—that's part of why I'm a geology major. Thankfully, I can get a job in a lab or something, 'cause I don't want to be out there anymore. That's partly why I'm in here, watching TV. I kind of feel like I have a bit of PTSD."

"Did it have glowing red eyes, like they had their own power source?"

Todd looked surprised. "Yes. Have you seen it?"

"I have," Bud answered. "What else can you add about it?"

"You saw it? Wow, I guess I'm not crazy after all, 'cause I'm the only one who actually saw anything, and nobody else believed me until we started hearing the howling. It was weird, like nothing I've ever heard. And we would hear something whacking on trees, way back in the forest. And one night, something really big picked up Allie's tent and dragged it across the clearing with her in it. That's our lab assistant. She actually left and went home. And Professor Cole was the one who had something throw rocks at his tent. It creeped us all out and we left the next morning."

"Was it black with thick shoulders?"

"Yes."

"I think what you and I both saw was someone in a costume, Todd. That's confidential, OK? But I found that costume later. I think it has something to do with Joe Swasey's murder. You have to keep this to yourself or it may harm my investigation, but I think it's safe to go out in the woods. That Bigfoot wasn't real."

Todd looked shocked. "A costume? Wow, what a great costume. I swear it looked real."

Bud could tell it would take Todd awhile to process this new information.

"Maybe you can still be a field geologist after all," Bud added.

Todd picked up the topo map and sat down on the edge of his bed.

"Wow. That's really weird, someone in a suit. A suit like that would be hard to make. How does it fit into the murder? I thought he'd been killed by the Bigfoot. They sure had me fooled. Guess there's a reason I'm not studying criminology."

"I think they're trying to scare people away from something, and Joe knew about it, so they killed him. Don't forget, that's confidential. By the way, do you know anything about what Professor Cole does on his days off?"

"Yeah, he runs around with some minerals guy doing mineral exploration. He works as a consultant. I think they might be looking for something like oil, I'm not sure."

"Oil? Is there oil up here?"

"There could very well be a few good pockets of it. Oil collects in anticlines, and the Swell is one big anticline."

"What's that?" Bud asked.

"It's where the earth has been folded up into a convex shape, it sort of swells up. That's why they call it the Swell, though it was actually pushed up. Sometimes they form big domes. That's why you have the Reef, it's where the forces pushed the sandstone almost straight up on the edge of the Swell. Usually it's from tectonic plate movement. The Swell was formed during the Laramide Orogeny. Orogeny means mountain building. It's the most recent one, the one that also pushed up the Rocky Mountains, maybe, though there's some who don't link the two."

He paused, then continued. "Anyway, oil often collects under anticlinal structures, because its buoyant and will rise up through the folds until something stops it, like a layer of impermeable sandstone or limestone. I think historically there has been some oil found up here, according to what Professor Cole told us. So that's what I'm thinking they're looking for—oil. Maybe gas. Or both."

Bud paused. There had been many lives lost for oil. He wondered if Joe Swasey's wasn't one.

"I would say you're about ready to graduate, Todd. You seem to really know your stuff. Have you ever heard of Mancos Resources?"

"Yeah, that's who the Prof's doing consulting for. We're not supposed to know anything, 'cause he signed a confidentiality statement with them. They figure if people find out what they're looking for, everyone will be out here."

"How do you know all that?"

"I saw their sign on an office building door in Price when we were coming through. *250 East Main, Mancos Resources, Inc. Mineral Exploration. Oil, Gas and Uranium.* I notice things like that 'cause I'm going to be a geologist, as soon as this class is done. I saw the same name on the door of the pickup the prof was in one afternoon when he came back to the cafe. I'm curious, so I asked him about it, and he told me he'd signed an agreement and couldn't talk about it."

Bud whistled. "I should've asked you from day one, Todd," he said. "I've been wondering about this since I first came up here. But one last question. Do you have any idea what the prof might have been looking for out at Joe's cabin? He was out there one time, but wouldn't tell me why."

"I dunno, Sheriff. Maybe Joe had something he wanted or wanted to see, at least. I hope he wasn't involved in all that. He's a really nice guy, kind of my mentor. In fact, he's the only reason I'm here in this class right now."

"How so?"

"I was flunking out. A lot of geology students really struggle with the physics and math, and I was one of them. Geology requires that you take classes in both, and in chemistry, too, and I was really discouraged. They're hard classes. I was ready to quit. He talked me out of it."

"That's great," Bud said. "And now that you know that Bigfoot's not real, you can carry on with your dreams."

22

Bud was on his way back down off the Swell when his radio crackled.

"Sheriff, this is Howie."

"10-4, go ahead."

"We have a problem here. Where are you?"

"I'm coming down off the Swell as we speak."

"I'm not sure what to do, Sheriff."

Bud wasn't either, until Howie told him what the problem was.

"What's the problem, Deputy?"

This caught Howie off-guard. Bud never called him deputy. Maybe he was going to get a raise or something.

"It's the trains."

"What trains?"

"Sheriff, you know what trains. Green River has trains, that's what trains."

Bud sighed.

"No, I know that, Howie, what about the trains is exactly the problem?"

"They seem to be stuck."

"Oh? How so?"

"They're not going anywhere."

"Why not?"

"Because they're stuck, that's the problem."

"OK, Howie, how about more details."

Bud was getting impatient. He'd already come several miles since the conversation started, and he was no farther ahead.

"You know the Amtrak, it comes in on the siding track," Howie paused for confirmation.

"I know."

"And there's always a big freight train that comes in ahead of it, going the opposite way. It just sits on the main track, or they call it a trunk, with its big engines, right immediately before the siding, letting Amtrak get in there, swing off the main trunk."

Bud replied, "Howie, your descriptive skills are way better than I thought. Go on."

Howie took this as a compliment, not getting the irony.

He continued, "Then the big freight train goes ahead, clearing the back track so Amtrak can continue back onto the main trunk from the siding after letting off or picking up passengers."

"Excellent. Go ahead." Maybe Howie's future lay in technical writing, Bud thought.

"Well, tonight the big freight train is just sitting there. It won't let Amtrak get out."

"There's probably something wrong with it, and it can't move."

"Well, Sheriff, I figured that was the case, and I agree with you one-hundred percent. Problem is, besides all those poor people sitting waiting on the train in those stuffy cars, problem is, it's blocking the road out to the airport."

"It will probably move soon, Howie, and the airport gets almost no business, so I think it will all work out."

"It's been over two hours already. There are people hanging around outside the Amtrak, but nobody knows what's going on."

"Did you ask them?"

"Not really, but it's pretty obvious."

"What about the engineer?"

"He's out walking the tracks. Last time I saw him, he was with two guys in bright orange vests, they looked like safety guys, and they were way way back towards the end of the train. It's a long train, too. They almost looked like little orange dots. I have no idea where the Amtrak conductor is, probably in the train taking a nap or reading train adventure magazines."

"Howie, I still don't see where it's a big problem. Nobody goes out to the airport very often. It's only got a few private planes."

"Well, Sheriff, it *is* a problem. I don't like to disagree with you, but we've got someone important coming in on a plane in about five minutes, and they won't be able to get into town."

"Who would that be?" Bud asked.

"A producer and director for CBS or NBC, I can't remember which. Maybe it was the Discovery Channel."

Bud smiled. Howie must not be easily impressed to not even remember who the big honchos worked for. Either that or he got really excited and didn't pay attention.

"Why are they coming to Green River?" He asked.

"To see you."

"Me?" Bud thought Howie was kidding. "Must be my new sunglasses," he said.

"Your what?" Howie asked.

"Never mind. Why are they coming to see me? Why am I just now finding this out, Howie?"

"I just learned it myself, Sheriff, so don't be mad at me."

"Who told you?"

"The secretary of whoever it is, can't remember. Something to do with TV."

Howie now thought this might be a good time to ask. "Say, Sheriff, Bud, would you have a problem if I got a little TV to watch in here when things are slow?"

"It's against state regulations," Bud answered. "Sorry, Howie."

"It's OK," Howie said, though his voice said different and that he was disappointed.

"Howie, back to these TV mystery persons. Why do they want to see me?"

"They said they're doing a special and want to interview you."

Bud sighed. He was nearly to Spotted Wolf Canyon.

"About what?"

"About seeing a Bigfoot. They're doing a Bigfoot special. Say, Sheriff, did you really see one?"

"No, and don't worry about the trains. Let the producer or whoever they are wait," Bud said, hoping they would get tired of waiting and go back to wherever.

He then added, "And if they want to see me, tell them I've gone missing. Something to do with a Bigfoot up on the Swell."

"Should I really tell them that?" Howie asked, incredulously.

"Yes."

"But it's not true."

"You actually don't know that, Howie. I'm up here on the Swell right now, and I'm not going to show up at the office, so as far as you're concerned, I've gone missing. 10-4, over."

Bud pulled off the freeway, taking the exit for the viewpoint and rest area just before the road dropped down through Spotted Wolf. Huge yellow signs commanded truckers to stop and check their brakes before proceeding down the five percent grade.

He got out of the Bronco and stood there awhile at the guardrail, taking in the view. It didn't matter how many times he saw the huge canyons and cliffs of the Reef, he was still impressed. It would take several lifetimes to explore them, unless you were a raven, he noted, as a pair flew over.

He thought of Millie. What in the world would possess Joe to kill ravens? They were amazing birds, supposedly the most intelligent of the bird species.

Just about then, a big truck pulled in behind him. It had the words Dino-Noble on its side. Larry swung down out of the big cab, and Bud noted he had a new cap on, one that read, *Utah Bigfoot Field Researcher*. Bud wondered where he'd got it.

"Hey, Bud, did you hear the news?"

"What news?" Bud replied.

"You know, the big news in Green River."

Bud was wondering if Larry hadn't been spending time with Howie.

"You mean about the trains?" Bud asked.

"What trains?"

Bud sighed. "Never mind. What news are you talking about?"

"Haven't you heard? Howie called up at the cafe, looking for you. They're doing a show about Bigfoot and want to interview you. Me, too."

"Why do *you* want to interview *me*?"

"No, no, they want to interview me, too."

Now Bud was beginning to think he himself had spent too much time around Howie, as it appeared he was beginning to think like him.

Larry added, "I'm headed that way with this load, going down to New Mexico. But I'm going to stop in town and meet the TV people. Are you coming?"

"I'll be along shortly," Bud replied. "But don't wait for me. And I don't think you're probably going to find any TV people around."

Larry nodded his head and swung back up into the truck. He sat there for a moment, then got back out.

"Bud, I need to talk to you about Millie. It's hard to do up at the cafe, 'cause she's always around, and I'm not sure it's really any of my business."

"What's going on, Larry?"

"She's been acting all weird. I dunno, maybe weird's not the word. Different. She's gone some, leaves me to watch the cafe for her, and I'm a heckuva bad cook. She's usually gone only for an hour or two, then she's back. This has been going on for a month or so. Then the other day she told me she's wanting to sell the cafe, start over someplace where it's green and civilized and there are people around. I told her that was fine, she should do it."

"Where would she go?" Bud asked.

"I dunno, Bud, but I know she has a son over in Colorado some place. But then she worried about those birds. Hellsbells, I told her, they're wild animals, they would adapt if she left, it would be just like before she came. There's only a half-dozen or so that even come over there for food. Then she worried about me, what would I do? I told her I'd saved enough and had been thinking about getting a little farm over by Elmo, and I'd be fine, I was tired of living in a motel anyway. I don't know what's going on, but it's not like her. She used to tell me she was gonna die with her feet in the Ghost Rock kitchen, cooking burgers."

Bud thought for a bit. He didn't know what to say. "Has anyone been coming around or anything? Anything different?"

"Well, yeah, Joe's gone now, that's different. She was taking off for a few hours here and there before he died, but it was just yesterday that she started talking about selling out. I would imagine Joe's death did something to her."

"Probably," Bud said. "Do you think she was going over to his cabin when she'd take off? Maybe she was seeing Joe."

"Hard to believe," Larry said. "She was always telling him to come in and take a shower in one of the rooms, and he chewed tobacco. She hated chew, said it was the most disgusting thing on earth. I can't imagine her wanting to hang out with him. He wasn't the cleanest thing on the planet, and Millie's into clean. I'm sure you've noticed the cafe is spotless."

Bud offered, "I wonder if the anonymous donation will help her out."

"You know, I don't know who gave it to her, but I imagine it will give her the means to leave if she decides to, which she didn't have before. It might make all the difference."

They said goodbye, and Bud followed Larry for a bit down the freeway, but the big truck had to go slow down that steep grade with its load, so Bud soon passed him.

He had no idea what was up with Millie. He had a strong urge to go out to Krider's new melon farm and just hang out for a bit, think about things, but he knew the melon farmer would still be out there.

Instead, he took the Hanksville exit at the bottom of the long grade and then turned left. He'd go back into the Morrison badlands, along the old Buckmaster Road. There wouldn't be anyone out there, and he could get some badly-needed solitude, maybe do a little rock hounding. He needed some time alone to think.

23

Just as Bud was about to get out of range of the Green River cell tower, his phone rang. It was his cousin Barry, who worked for the power company over in the little town of Ridgway, Colorado. Barry had no formal training in forensics, but he'd been elected county coroner over there and had learned quite a bit on his own.

Barry said, "Hey, cousin, how's everything over in Green River country? I have some news for you."

Bud had sent Barry the hair sample he'd collected from the Bigfoot suit, even though he knew his cousin was busy. He needed some help sleuthing, and Barry was always saying to call him if he ever needed anything. He'd hated to ask for help, but it looked now like maybe Barry had come up with something.

"Did you find out anything about the suit?" Bud asked eagerly.

"I did, but it's not really about the hair itself. I really didn't know what to do with that one, Bud. I thought about sending it in to the Colorado Bureau of Investigation, but it just didn't make sense. I knew they would just tell me, yup, it's hair from a suit. So I tried another tack."

"How so?" asked Bud.

"Well, I did some research, and I found out that historically, all the good gorilla suits were made in or near Hollywood, which makes sense—you know, *Planet of the Apes* and all that. So, I started calling around, and I found a couple of places, and I asked for hair samples. They each sent me one, then I matched them up with a little help from my forensic buddies at the CBI. Sure enough, both companies used the same material, so I had to try something different, but that at least let me know I was on the right track."

He continued. "I then asked them to tell me of any suit shipments they'd made to Utah. At first, they didn't want to release any information, so I had to pull rank a bit, but I finally got a list from each of them. Not much of a list. Seems gorilla suits aren't a big item in Utah, for some reason or other. One company had sold a suit to some amusement park up in Salt Lake City, and that was it. The other place had sold one to some guy in Salina, which isn't far from your neck of the woods, is it?"

"Nope, it's just over the hill a hundred miles," Bud replied. A picture was starting to form on his mind's TV, and it had Jimmy Wilson front and center. "How much was the suit?"

"These things aren't cheap. The guy spent $2,000 on it."

"Whoeee," Bud whistled through his teeth. "Did you get a name?"

"No. I tried, but they said it had been shipped to one of those private mailbox places there. When I called them, they said they didn't have a name, it was some outfit called Swell Films. Sounds like an indie movie company to me."

Bud expressed his appreciation for the information, visited awhile about family, then they hung up.

He sat there in his old Bronco. It appeared that someone had tried to hide their tracks, but having the suit shipped to Salina was a big tip off. It had to be Jimmy Wilson, as he was from Salina, or someone who was working with him, maybe even Professor Cole. He turned the ignition key and drove on through the big Morrison hills and Buckmaster Draw.

The dirt road wound around the front of the candy-cane colored hills, with a little two-track occasionally taking off up to some old long-abandoned uranium mine. Bud loved this country, in spite of its desolation, or maybe because of its desolation. There was never anyone out here, except the occasional rock hound.

And Jimmy Wilson.

If he were writing a book, thought Bud, nobody would believe it, he'd have to change the plot a little. He had just got a call about the Bigfoot suit, making Jimmy Wilson a prime suspect, and now here was Jimmy, right here. But truth is stranger than fiction, he thought.

Jimmy was up on a hill poking around, and for once, his dogs weren't with him. He was now driving a white GMC, and this truck had "Mancos Resources, Inc." painted on the door, with an atomic symbol where the O should be in the word *Mancos*. Jimmy appeared to be looking for something.

He saw Bud and came sliding down the slope, digging his boot heels into the soft clays.

"Afternoon, Sheriff," Jimmy said cordially, touching the brim of his old beat-up cowboy hat.

"Hello, Jimmy. Nice day to be out rock hounding."

Bud decided to pretend he thought Jimmy was just out kicking around, though he knew better.

"It is a nice day, but I'm not rock hounding, Sheriff, I'm working."

"Working? Oh. Well, it appears you and the prof are both working for Mancos, and I already know you can't talk about it, so I'll save my breath."

Jimmy grinned. "You're catching on, Sheriff."

"I am," Bud smiled back. "And I'm beginning to think you boys are out looking for oil. Am I right?"

"Dang it, Sheriff, you sure are persistent."

"I'm the sheriff. That's part of my job. That and being thorough. And I know the Swell could potentially have some big finds. It's an anticline, and anticlines often mean petroleum resources." Bud was feeling a bit like a geologist, recalling what Todd had told him. "Speaking of thorough, do you know anything about a big black gorilla suit that was modified by someone into a Bigfoot suit?"

Jimmy looked puzzled. "No."

"You're aware that I was visited by someone wearing that suit just before you and the prof showed up at Swasey's cabin that night, aren't you?"

"No."

"That suit was shipped to Salina, Jimmy, your hometown. Why don't you tell me why you ordered an expensive Bigfoot suit and then had someone scare the bejeebers out of everyone on the Swell, including me? You were trying to scare them away, because you and the prof were on the verge of finding something up there, something worth big bucks, and my guess goes to some kind of oil something or other. The prof pretended to not be in on it and let your Bigfoot lackey scare his students so badly one of them left. I'm going to guess that Mancos Resources bought you that suit, 'cause I know you don't have that kind of money. Am I right?"

"No, and why would the prof be scaring his own students? Why not just find some excuse to call off the field school?"

"Because he needed to be out there so he could work with you."

Bud changed the subject. He still had some things to think out. "Do you know that a TV production company is in Green River this very moment to do a special on Bigfoot sightings on the Swell?"

Jimmy looked genuinely surprised. "No."

Bud stopped. He was running out of steam.

Jimmy said, "Bud, you're wrong on all counts. I had nothing to do with a Bigfoot suit or anything like that, and we haven't found anything at all up there. That's why I'm down here. The prof is a good guy, and he would never lie to his students like that. He's up there working with them right now, when he could've taken another day off to make some good money working with me."

"And Sheriff," he added. "I myself saw a Bigfoot up there. It was two years ago, long before any of this was going on. I'll tell you about it someday, but it scared me so bad I won't go around up there alone. I always have my dogs with me, if not another person. And my cousin Henry has seen one. In fact, he thinks one's eaten some of his cattle. And I could name you a few other people who heard some pretty weird things up there. This was all long before some bozo was wandering around in a suit. In fact, how do you know it was a suit and not a real Bigfoot?"

"I can't tell you," Bud replied, kind of enjoying throwing some of Jimmy's medicine back at him. "It's confidential and would be against the law for me to discuss it. By the way," he added, "Just what exactly are you looking for out here in dino bone country?"

"I can't tell you," Jimmy grinned, then turned and got into his truck, leaving Bud in the dust.

24

It was late afternoon when Bud pulled into the small parking lot of the Emery County Sheriff's Office, Howie's cruiser also there.

Across Main Street and a few blocks back, Bud could see that Amtrak was still sitting at the station, with another longer freight train blocking the main line. It appeared they hadn't fixed whatever the problem was.

He wondered if the Green River motels might be full of train travelers tonight—either that or the Greyhound Bus was going to get some business.

Howie seemed glad enough to see him, but his face was red and he looked upset.

"Sheriff, I'm truly glad to see you. We have to do something about those dang trains!"

"Why, Howie?" Bud asked.

"Because the TV people are stuck over there. We need to help them out. They're going to spend a lot of money here if this thing goes. It's called economic development."

Bud conceded that Howie had a point, then added that there was nothing they could do, except send them around on the old highway, where they could come out by the Hatt Ranch on the Hanksville road, then get on the freeway back to Green River. It was a good 30 miles, though, partly on a rough road.

Howie picked up the phone, repeated what Bud had told him, then hung up.

"I wish I'd known that a long time ago," he said a bit sullenly.

"Look, Howie, it's really not our job to make sure some TV honchos can get into town. Where did they get a vehicle, anyway? Didn't you say they flew in? There's no car rental place around here."

"They're expecting their own car to come in later, but until then, they're borrowing Sammy's pickup," Howie answered. Sammy was the caretaker at the airport. He also did mechanical work when a plane needed it and air traffic control, which is what he called turning on the airport lights at night.

"Well, that old highway's pretty rough, half potholes. The county hasn't maintained it for years. I hope they make it OK. They could potentially get lost, though it would be hard to do."

Bud kind of enjoyed the visual of a bunch of TV bigwigs in Sammy's old beat-up truck.

"They'll be OK," Howie assured him. "Sammy's driving."

"Why didn't Sammy mention that back route to them before this? He knows about it."

"Probably 'cause he's driving and doesn't want to tear his truck all to heck," Howie answered.

"His truck's already torn all to heck. But you're right, they'll be fine. I wonder who told them there had been Bigfoot sightings up on the Swell."

"Wasn't me. This is the first I've heard of them."

"Well, I'm gonna call it a day and go on home, Howie."

"I guess since those TV people won't be getting in here anytime soon, I'll go, too," Howie answered, wishing again he was sheriff and could just wander around wherever and whenever he wanted.

Bud left, and Howie lingered a bit, thinking about what he would do if this were his office. He'd get a small TV, to heck with state regs, he'd hide it in a cupboard or something.

He might even get a little toaster oven, as he was getting tired of eating across the street at Howie's every day. He'd been there, done that, too many years, for sure.

He turned out the lights and locked the door, heading to Jay's Tavern for dinner.

~

B ud decided to swing by Prof Krider's melon farm on his way home. He was really toying with the idea of having a new job, and it had really helped his outlook ever since the prof had mentioned it.

He drove on past the bungalow, noting that Wilma Jean was home, and then on out to the farm. He pulled over under a big cottonwood tree, got out, and leaned against the Bronco, listening to a meadowlark singing.

Bud whistled back, and soon he and the bird were calling to each other. Bud prided himself on some of his bird whistles. He'd learned them as a kid, and he even knew a bunch of raven calls. This made him think again of Joe Swasey, and he really just wanted to stop thinking of Joe.

He needed a vacation, he knew that. It had been a long time since he and Wilma Jean had gone anywhere for more than a day or so, and that was over to Ridgway to visit his cousin Barry. Maybe he could arrange some time off when he had the Swasey case closed—if he ever did.

Now Bud felt a bit ashamed again. He was out here, hiding out, and he knew it. He didn't want to deal with reality anymore. This case was really getting to him. He thought he'd figured some of it out with Jimmy buying the Bigfoot costume, but apparently not, though Jimmy could well be lying.

Bud now sat down under the big tree with his back against the trunk. He started thinking back to when he was a kid, growing up in Price. He'd spent a lot of time on his uncle's farm, helping him irrigate the alfalfa, prune the fruit trees, milk the cows. It all sounded idyllic now and far away.

He'd wanted to someday be a farmer, just like his uncle, but life had interfered. He'd graduated high school and married Wilma Jean, his high-school sweetheart. He'd then gone to work in the uranium mines, just like his dad.

Now Bud was starting to nod off a bit. He was getting sleepy, and he thought maybe he should get back home before he just flat out drifted off out there. It was such a peaceful place, and now that meadowlark was back.

Suddenly, Bud sat up straight, his back stiff. He stood up and got into his Bronco. Why hadn't he seen it before, since it was right in front of his eyes? If it had been a snake, it would've bit him.

Uranium. That's what the prof and Jimmy were searching for, uranium. The Swell had been the site of a number of producing mines that had all shut down during the last bust, the same one that had put him out of work and eventually led to him being sheriff. Since then, things had turned around, and there was talk of reopening the mill down in Radium. That meant the mines would reopen. And he'd heard the price of uranium ore was getting back up there again, making exploration feasible.

He knew he'd solved part of the riddle, but he wasn't sure if it was an important part or not. What did it have to do with Joe Swasey? Joe knew every inch of the Swell, and maybe he'd been helping them out. Maybe he knew something they didn't want him to talk about. But what did that have to do with the buried paintings? And Joe's fear of a Bigfoot killing him? And who was in that Bigfoot suit?

He needed to get back up to the Ghost Rock Cafe and talk to Roger and take a look at Joe's rock collection. Maybe that would give him some answers. He'd get up there first thing tomorrow, but for now, he just wanted to get some rest, see Wilma Jean, Hoppie, and little Pierre, who he'd barely got to know. He started the Bronco and went on home, noting the lightning on the horizon, way up on the Swell.

25

Bud sat in his big chair, feet up on the desk, watching the action across the street at Howie's. Apparently the owner was gone, because a girl and a boy, both who looked to be in their late teens, were chasing each other around the outside of the building, carrying what looked like water bottles and squirting each other. He knew they were employees, as he'd sat and watched the place before when he was bored, but it wasn't usually this entertaining.

The girl was now standing in front of the building, peeking around the corner. Bud had a good view of the place and could see all but the back. That's where he figured the guy must be, because he couldn't see him.

Now he saw the guy sneak up behind the girl, indeed coming from the back of the building. She saw him at the last minute and ran, but not before he managed to get her with his water bottle, not squirting her, but throwing the whole bottle at her.

She went into the building while the guy hid again in back. Bud could see through the big plate glass windows, and she was getting something. She then went around to the back, and he could now see the guy running, soaked with water.

Bud started laughing.

Just then, a customer drove up, and the pair quickly went inside.

Ah, to be young again, Bud thought. He remembered a similar time when he'd been rafting with Wilma Jean and they'd had a big water fight which left them both in the river, the raft drifting on down to who knows where, as they never saw it again. Good times, he thought, except that same night when he'd had to explain the missing raft to its owner, his friend Jack. That water fight ended up costing him fifty dollars, big bucks back then, when he was still in high school.

Now Bud decided he'd go get a milkshake across the street at Howie's instead of going to his regular, the Chow Down. He needed to spend the day in the office for once, so he'd sent Howie up to the Ghost Rock Cafe to poke around and look for clues, instead of going himself. Bud thought it would do him some good to go see the place and meet everyone. Besides, Bud wanted to be alone. He had a few calls to make. He would go up there himself soon enough.

Howie had wanted to stay in Green River in case the TV people showed up, but Bud convinced him they might never show up. Maybe they'd decided to go down to Hanksville instead. So far, he hadn't seen a soul—he had no idea where they were.

Bud stood and looked across Main Street and on over to the tracks. It appeared that the trains had finally got their act together, because they were now both gone.

One of the calls Bud wanted to make was to the forensics lab up in Salt Lake. He wanted to know what was taking so long for them to analyze Joe's ashes, as he'd sent them right after getting them from Doc Richardson.

He called and was told they'd had to send them off to a lab in D.C. because of what they'd found. They wanted to be sure, as it was rare. They would probably know the results in a few days or so.

Bud wondered what that was all about, but they wouldn't tell him over the phone. There was no way to prove he was who he said he was, and it was a policy they had. He would have to wait.

He walked across the street and ordered a vanilla milkshake, sitting down where he could see his office—that way, he'd know if someone came in.

Bud hadn't been there long when a big black Land Rover drove up next to the drive-in. It had to be Doc Richardson, Bud thought, and sure enough, the doctor got out and came inside Howie's. He seemed a bit surprised to see Bud sitting there.

"Hello, Bud," he said in his soft voice. Everyone loved Doc Richardson, he had such a gentle bedside manner.

"Hi, Doc. Good to see you. You slumming today?"

Doc laughed. "This is my day to work at the clinic."

Bud knew the doc volunteered at the rural clinic here one day a month. He also volunteered at several other clinics around the region. It was his way of being charitable.

"Let me buy you lunch, Doc."

"Thanks, but I'm just getting some coffee. I have to get over there pretty soon."

He got a cup of coffee and sat down by Bud.

"You still working on Joe Swasey's case?"

Bud said he was, kind of, anyway, wondering why the doc asked.

"I still think it was an animal, Bud. Say, I have some news. It's kind of sad."

"What's that?"

"Joanne and I are splitting up. I'm going to move back to Colorado, give her the house, try to start a new life."

Bud was shocked. The doc represented security to him with his nice brick house up in Price and lovely wife, even if it was a lifestyle that only a doctor can maintain—black Land Rovers and all that.

"I'm really sorry to hear that, Doc. Is there anything I can do?"

"No, but thanks. I'm already packed to go. This is my next to last day as a doctor in Carbon and Emery counties. I'm leaving in three days."

"Doc, you're going to really be missed around here, let me tell you. I wish you all the best and hope you'll come back to visit. Let me know if there's anything I can do."

"If you figure out how to fix a torn heart, Sheriff, give me a call. Say, was the money helpful to Millie?"

"Of course it was. She almost started crying. But I didn't say a word, that's between you and me and the bedpost."

"Thanks. And about that donation for the new vehicle, any idea yet what you'll get?"

"I was wishing for a black Land Rover," Bud joked. "Actually, it may end up that we get a Toyota of some kind. We're doing some research."

"That sounds good, Bud." Doc stood, saying, "Well, wish me luck," and with that, he reached down, shook Bud's hand, then walked out the door.

Bud followed him out. This was a sad piece of news. He again wished the doc good luck.

"Say, Doc," he asked, running his finger through the dust on doc's Land Rover. "It looks like black might not be the best color for working in the backcountry. It really shows the dirt, doesn't it?"

"It does, and I wouldn't get black again. I just came across the Swell. I spent the morning over in Salina. They sometimes call me to come in when they get short handed. Well, good luck to you, too, Bud, and enjoy your new rig, whatever you end up with."

They shook hands again and parted ways, but for some reason, Bud had a hunch he'd see Doc Richardson again.

Bud was sitting at his desk, thinking about Doc Richardson and what Krider had said about those who have the most to lose being the most fearful. It looked like the doc wasn't in that category anymore, he thought, since his ex-wife was going to get it all. He rubbed the bridge of his nose. He was losing one of his prime suspects.

The phone rang.

"Sheriff's office, Bud."

"Sheriff, it's Roger."

"Oh, hello, Rog. I was up there yesterday and tried to find you. Everything OK?"

"Sheriff, no. Your deputy's up here, but I don't think he's really going to be much help, 'cause all he can do is pace around. I think you need to come up. Bud, something's happened to Millie. She's missing."

"What? For how long?"

"The cafe was never closed up last night, so it would have to be sometime after about four in the afternoon, 'cause that's when I was in there last. I hope she's OK. Her car's still here. Larry's still gone on a truck run, as far as I can tell."

"I'll be right there," Bud said, hanging up, then dialing Howie.

"Howie, it's Bud. What's going on?"

"Millie's missing," he answered in a voice that said he might be considering the restaurant business again.

"Do you know anything?"

"No."

"OK, Howie, you come on back and cover for me at the office. I'm going to lock it up and head up there."

"10-4 and over," Howie said, sounding relieved as he hung up the phone.

At this rate, his old Bronco was going to wear out before he could get a new vehicle, Bud thought as he locked the office door and headed once again up the Swell.

Bud thought he saw Howie's car at about Spotted Wolf, which meant Howie was wasting no time getting back to the office.

The old Bronco slowed as they climbed the stiff grade. He was beginning to feel at home up here, and it wasn't particularly where he wanted to feel at home, as he preferred Green River.

He soon pulled into the cafe's parking lot and went inside. It appeared that the entire geology class was there, along with Professor Cole, waiting for Bud to give them their marching orders. They wanted to find Millie.

He quickly ascertained the situation, deciding there wasn't much to ascertain. No one had seen Millie since about four yesterday, the cafe was left open, her car was still here, she wasn't in the little trailer behind the motel where she lived, and her ravens were hanging around, waiting to be fed.

Bud wasn't sure where to start looking, but he had a hunch—Joe's cabin.

"Is there anything we can do to help?" Professor Cole asked.

"Professor, I appreciate the offer, but I think it might lead to more problems. I'm going to take Roger with me and go look, and if we need to, we'll call Search and Rescue. I know you guys are about as competent as it gets in the backcountry, but we don't know yet what's going on. We don't need any more missing persons up here, nor do we need anyone harmed."

"Do you suspect foul play?" Roger asked.

"It's the first thing the law thinks of, Roger. We're trained that way. But it doesn't mean it happened. We just need to be cautious."

Professor Cole called the students together and instructed everyone to go to their rooms or the cafe and stay there.

Bud pulled Roger aside.

"Rog, I have a hunch. Let's go over to your room and look around real quick before we go to the cabin."

"OK, I can show you Joe's rock collection."

They went into Roger's room, which was basically stacked with rocks in every possible nook and cranny.

"Did you find any of interest?" Bud asked, smiling, thinking of his own rockhounding tendencies to pick up everything he saw.

"All of them," Roger grinned.

"Rog, would you know uranium minerals if you saw them?"

"I would, and that's just what I was going to tell you. Joe had some stuff so good I know it's radioactive as all heck. Looks like carnotite and uranitite. Very nice samples."

"Are you keeping them in here? I hope not. And I hope you didn't mention them to Professor Cole."

"No, they're out back behind the motel. I can show them to you, and Professor Cole doesn't know about any of this, as per your orders. But first, take a look at these Fremont pots. There's two of them. Both worth some good money, Sheriff, and I'm wondering where Joe got them. I hid them right here behind the little heater, wrapped in towels."

Roger leaned over, looking behind the room's space heater. He stood back up stiffly.

"They're gone! How can they be gone? Nobody's been in here, and Millie was the only other one who knew about them..."

"Rog, I think we need to get out to the cabin. I think those pots are related to everything, and Millie might be in serious danger, assuming she's still alive."

They ran and jumped into the Bronco, Roger checking to make sure his little .22 pistol was in its holster inside his jacket, while Bud thought about the big wad of bills he'd so casually handed Millie in the cafe.

They were soon at Swasey's cabin, looking around.

"Look, Bud, you go that way, over by where the ATV road comes up, and I'll go over by the alcove. Let's stay within yelling distance of one another." Roger was taking over his job, Bud thought, and doing a good job of it, too.

Bud walked to the edge of the canyon where the ATV trail led up from the bottom. Eagle Canyon had long ago eroded out here enough to be passable, and a band of detritus fallen from the cliffs provided enough room for an ATV to climb up from the canyon.

He looked around, but saw nothing. The dirt was soft enough that if someone had walked down here, he would see tracks.

He decided to go on down into the canyon. The bottom wasn't that far down, maybe fifty feet or so. He followed the trail on down, searching all around. Nothing.

He walked for a bit, wondering where Millie was. Now he could hear Roger yelling. How did he get down into the canyon, Bud wondered.

He yelled back, then walked in the direction of the sound, but Roger wasn't there. He decided to call him on his cell phone, but discovered there was no service down in the canyon.

Now Roger was calling Bud's name again, and he was further away. It was kind of eerie, Bud thought.

And he now recalled the dream he'd had where the voice was calling him away from Joe. He felt a chill, even though it was broad daylight.

"Roger!" he called.

"Bud!" he heard Roger's voice again, though now further away, and it didn't sound quite right. "Bud!"

Dang, this was spooky. "Roger! Where are you?"

He had decided to turn back when he heard his name called again, but this time right above him. He looked up.

It was Millie. She sat in a small alcove a good twenty feet above him in the cliffs. How she got up there, he had no idea.

"Oh my God, Bud," she was crying. "I'm stuck up here. Thank God you're here."

Her voice had drifted with the wind, sounding like it was moving, Bud thought, relieved.

"Stay right there, I'm going for help."

Now Millie became hysterical. "No! No! You can't leave. No!"

"I have to get help. I can't get you down by myself, Millie. We need a rope. It's OK, I'll be right back."

She started crying and almost wailing, "No! No!"

Bud sat down. "OK, Millie, I'll stay here. Roger will figure it out and find me. He'll track me down here."

He had no sooner said it than Roger stood there, saying he'd heard Bud calling him and asking if he'd seen Millie.

Bud just pointed up.

27

It was the first time Bud had been in Millie's little trailer, and he was favorably impressed. It was old, but had warm blonde-wood walls that he suspected were the original beechwood used in trailers of a long-gone era. Millie had Navajo rugs on the floors and a few photos of the canyons hanging on the walls. The place was downright cozy.

It was then that Bud noticed the small painting above the blonde-wood desk in the corner. It was of a Fremont pot, beautifully done, surrounded by purple-blue canyon sweetpea.

He got up and looked closer. Sure enough, Joe Swasey's signature was in the corner.

He looked at Millie. She was curled up on the couch with a warm blanket wrapped around her, drinking hot cider. Roger sat next to her, his arm around her shoulder, consoling her. She was trying to stifle sobs. Bud thought that maybe she was still in shock.

She noticed Bud looking at the painting and stopped sobbing long enough to say, "It's the last one, as far as I know."

"You might want me to take that down to Green River and put it in the evidence safe," he answered. "Where it will be safe."

"Yes, I think you should," she answered, subdued. "What talent that man had, all gone. So gone." She broke into sobs again.

"Millie, can you tell us what happened?" Roger asked. "If it's too soon, it's OK."

"Don't leave me here alone, please don't. Will you guys stay here with me tonight?" She sounded downright panicked. "That thing is still out there. Oh my God." Now she was sobbing again.

Roger tried again. "Millie, did something try to harm you out there?"

Millie stopped sobbing. "I'm going to try to control myself. I'm OK, now, but just don't leave."

Bud looked at Roger, who replied, "Millie, I'll stay here with you tonight, don't worry."

Millie now quieted, sipping her cider a bit. Roger asked. "Was it cold out there, Millie?"

For some reason, Bud got the feeling that Roger had been trained in how to interview people. He'd have to ask him about it later, but he was using techniques Bud had learned in law enforcement—make the person feel safe and like you identify with them. But maybe it was just because Roger did identify with Millie.

Millie now started talking more freely. "It was all those damned pots."

"Where are the pots now?" Bud asked.

"I put them back where Joe said he got them. In that alcove I was in."

"They're up there?" Roger asked. "I didn't see any pots when I rappeled down there to help you, Millie."

"That's because I buried them."

"Oh. Why?"

"Because it was bad luck to have them. I didn't want anything to happen to you, like it did Joe."

"Joe had pots?"

"Yes."

"You mean, besides these?"

"Yes."

"Where did he get them?"

"I don't know. OK, I do know, kind of. From all over. He would go out and find the pots and then do paintings of them. I was helping him. I saw what talent he had, and I would get him art supplies in town. I encouraged him to paint them. I didn't want to tell anyone when we talked about Joe earlier. His death was all my fault."

"How could that be, Millie?" Bud asked quietly.

"Because if he hadn't been selling the paintings, he wouldn't have been killed. I know it." She started sobbing again.

"Why was he killed?" Roger asked.

"I don't know, but I know it had something to do with the pots."

"What happened to the pots after he painted them?"

"He said he took them back to where he found them and reburied them."

"Reburied them? He must've been grave digging. Did anyone else know what he was doing?" Roger asked.

"Not that I know of. I didn't even tell Larry. I think I was the only one who knew he would find pots and paint them. He knew every square inch of this country, and he told me there was stuff out there way more amazing than any Fremont pot."

"Did he ever say what?"

"No. But he was scared to go out at night. He said there were Bigfoot out there, and he was getting ready to leave the Swell. After last night, so am I."

Roger took Millie's empty cup and refilled it with more cider.

"Tell us what happened, Millie. Tell us about last night. And don't worry, I'm going to stay here with you all night."

It was now dark, and Bud was wondering if he would ever get home. He felt a bit guilty, like he should stay here with Roger, but was torn. For a brief second, he pictured Krider's melon farm.

Finally, he said, "Millie, I'm staying, too. Not to worry."

She continued. "Thanks, guys. I took the pots, it was late afternoon, and you were gone, Roger, out in the field, I guess. I used my master key to get into your room, and I put the pots in a little backpack. I knew where Joe had got them, because he told me. We had hiked down there a couple of times together."

She continued, sipping her hot cider. "I was going to go down into the canyon, but something felt odd. I felt like I was being followed. So, instead of going down, I decided to go up. I kind of circled around up on top. I could see down to where the alcove was, below me."

That explained why he hadn't found any tracks, Bud thought. Not her tracks, anyway. Roger had pointed out a couple of tracks to him on their way out, but no way were they Millie's.

"I decided to just shimmy down into the alcove from above. There were a couple of junipers I could grab onto. I did that, and I ended up tearing them off, they weren't very big. It had rained a bit last night and was slick. I managed to slide down into the alcove, and thankfully not off the edge on down the cliff, or I wouldn't be talking to you right now. I know it was stupid, but I was scared. Something was following me. And then, I was stuck."

"Did you see what was following?" Bud asked.

"No, I saw only its outline in the shadows, but it was huge. It stood below me and tried to climb up and get to me. It did this all night, and the sounds it made, oh my God." She started weeping again. "I'm leaving this place as soon as I can."

"Millie," Bud asked. "Would you believe it's somebody in a suit? I saw it myself out there one night. Darn scary."

"Bud, this wasn't a suit. Nobody on this planet could make a suit like that."

"Do you have any idea who killed Joe?" He thought he would try again.

"No, I really don't. But I want to sleep now, forget all this. I'm going to sleep now."

Bud was tired, and he knew Roger was, too. Millie refused to sleep alone in her bedroom, so she slept on the couch. Roger got a little rollaway from the motel and put it in the adjacent kitchen, and Bud would sleep in Millie's room. Millie propped a big chair against the front door, even though it was locked.

Bud called Wilma Jean to tell her the latest. She said she would turn the porch light off, and hoped no Bigfoot were down her way. Bud assured her it was a man in a suit, but he himself wondered, after Roger described the prints he'd found. They didn't match the foot on the stick, and they sank deep into the ground, like something that weighed at least six or seven hundred pounds.

Later, Bud dreamt again that something was calling him, and when he woke, something rustled outside. He decided it was the wind and went back to sleep, but with his gun handy.

28

Bud woke up, disoriented, with no idea where he was. It was pitch dark, and he could hear a low murmuring sound. He lay there for a bit, quiet, when it finally came to him. He was in Millie's trailer. But why was it so dark? And what was that sound?

He slipped off the bed, carefully placing his feet on the floor in the dark. He'd slept with his clothes on, even his boots, so he'd be ready for anything. He felt a bit headachy.

He quietly stood, getting his bearings, a bit dizzy. The murmurings were louder now. He reached around a bit in the dark and found the doorknob, carefully and quietly opening it. Light streamed in, and he was blinded for a moment.

He could now hear voices, and it sounded like Roger and someone else he recognized but couldn't quite place. He opened the door all the way.

It was broad daylight. Millie must have some kind of window covers that kept out the light. Maybe she was a light sleeper.

He had overslept and gotten too much sleep, which left him groggy. He needed coffee.

Roger was sitting on Millie's couch and greeted Bud, then Bud saw Todd standing in the doorway.

"Where's Millie?" Bud asked.

"At the cafe," Roger said. "Hey, Sheriff, Todd here has something he'd like to share with you."

"Oh, man, I hope it's not something that requires thinking," Bud replied. "I can't believe how late I slept."

"Yeah, Millie said she's acquired insomnia since Joe's death. She covered all her bedroom windows. Did you hear something messing around the trailer last night?"

"I thought I was dreaming."

"You weren't. I went outside and looked, but didn't see anything."

"This place is getting creepier and creepier," said Todd. "I'm about ready to leave." He continued. "I found something you might be interested in, Sheriff," pulling a plastic sandwich baggie out of his pocket.

He added, "It was over by Swasey's cabin. I'm still working on that outcropping over there, but I'm kind of getting scared of the place."

Bud studied the package. Inside was a small silver cross. It was ornate and a bit tarnished, but fine silversmithing. It looked old, like possibly a family heirloom, and maybe made of silver with a touch of copper—Mexican silver.

"Thanks, Todd. Nice work. Tell the prof I don't want anyone around that area. Where exactly was it?"

"Over in an alcove near the cabin. The alcove's hidden behind some thorn bushes."

"I know that alcove," Bud said. "Where about in the alcove exactly?"

"Just right there, lying kind of over in the corner. And there was trash in there, too."

"What kind of trash?"

"Food wrappers."

"OK. Todd, thanks again. Oh yes, I've been wanting to ask you, did you ever see any horse hoof prints over there around the cabin or in that area at all?"

Todd thought for a moment. "Not that I recall."

"Nothing?"

"Nope. But we've had a little rain and wind."

"Were you eating a hamburger by any chance when you found Joe? And maybe left part of it there?"

"No."

"OK, thanks. I'm gonna go get some coffee over at the cafe."

"We'll join you, if that's OK," Roger said.

"Of course it's OK."

As they walked to the cafe, Bud noticed that high above, the sky was filled with ravens. There must be at least fifty or more up there. They stopped to watch the birds as they circled, riding the air currents high above.

"Buzzards," Roger proclaimed.

Bud looked harder. Yes, buzzards. He could now tell, looking closer. Buzzards dipped their wings differently than ravens and seemed to be more tippy and lighter, although they were actually bigger birds.

"Must be migrating through," Bud said. "It's that time of year." Where they were going he had no idea, but every spring they came through, though they usually were down in Green River, hanging out by the river. He'd seen them roosting in the big cottonwoods down there, sometimes by the dozens.

Bud came around to the front of the cafe, only to see a big black Land Rover parked there. At first, he thought it must be Doc Richardson, but then he realized this particular Land Rover was a bit longer than the doc's—in fact, a lot longer. It was a stretch Rover. Bud had never seen such a thing. He noticed it was all dusty.

Millie greeted them as they walked in. She seemed to have recovered from her adventure and looked like nothing had happened.

Bud was a bit irritated, because whoever owned the stretch Land Rover had taken the back booth, where he always sat. There were three of them, two men and a woman. Bud and the guys sat down in a front booth instead.

Millie came over. "Hey guys, thanks for everything. Breakfast on the house. You, too, Todd. Did you guys notice anything different?"

"Buzzards," Bud replied.

Millie looked irritated. "Well, those buzzards are going to make me rich, I hope so, anyway."

"How so?" Bud was perplexed and wondered why she was irritated.

"They're going to do a movie about the Bigfoot up here. I already talked to them about it. They want to interview me, and they're going to pay me $500 for it. I might even be in the movie, talking and everything, and then I get more, though I have to join some actor's union."

Roger and Todd looked amused. Bud laughed.

"Millie, the buzzards I was referring to are outside. They're migrating through."

She ran out to look, then came back in, all excited. "Hey you all back there, you might want some of this for your movie."

The trio jumped up and ran outside.

"We can just make our own breakfast," Bud said. "We don't have food-handler's licenses, but I don't think the sheriff is going to arrest us. Otherwise, we're going to starve to death while Millie shows off the buzzards."

"If we starve, she can start feeding the buzzards along with the ravens," Roger said.

"Only in the wilds of Utah would someone think buzzards are cool," Todd said. "Even though I personally like them myself."

They went into the kitchen and made eggs and toast while drinking coffee and talking about the odds of being discovered by Hollywood on the Swell, of all places.

29

Bud was on his way down off the Swell and almost at Spotted Wolf when, sure enough, Howie called on the radio.

"Sheriff, we got a problem."

"What's up, Howie?"

"It looks like we're in for some flooding. The river is bankfull. You still up on the Swell? Maybe we should open a branch office up there. We could call it the Swell Sheriff. Or how about the Sheriff's Swell Office."

"Howie, that's very funny," Bud said, though he really didn't think it was funny at all. "Does it look like we maybe need to start evacuating things?"

"I'm not sure, Sheriff."

"Cover for me. I'm on my way."

"As usual, 10-4."

Bud wasn't sure if he meant the 10-4 was as usual or the covering for him, but he suspected the latter. Howie seemed to be getting more relaxed, and he wasn't sure if that was good or bad. Given that Howie had been almost cowering when he first started the job, Bud decided it was good.

Bud was standing on the bridge, looking down into the river, wondering how much higher it might get, when a vehicle drove up behind him and stopped, right in the middle of the lane.

It was normal for Green Riverites to meet each other on the roads and just stop to talk through their car windows, but the bridge might not be such a good place, Bud thought.

He turned. It was a black stretch Land Rover.

"Is it going to flood?"

The back window was open, and Bud recognized the guy talking as one of the TV people he'd seen at the Ghost Rock Cafe. The guy was tanned and wore what looked to be a brand-new white Stetson. Bud wondered if that was to make people think he was a good guy.

Bud answered, "It's bankfull. It will flood if it gets any higher."

"Can we come out on the middle of the bridge here and set up some cameras?"

"Probably not a good idea."

"OK, how about next to the bridge?"

"Not my call 'cause it's private land."

"Who owns it?"

"The State of Utah. Educational Trust Lands."

"The state? Why would they care?"

"I didn't say they would care, I just don't have the authority to give you permission. Why do you want to film the river if you're doing a Bigfoot film?"

"Drama. We're into drama."

Bud noted that a few cars were waiting behind the limo.

"Better get going, you're blocking traffic."

The guy saluted him and told the driver to move 'em on out. It reminded Bud of an old TV show he used to watch called *Rawhide*, about a perpetual cattle drive where the hero, a cowboy named Rowdy, was always telling everyone to move 'em on out.

Maybe the director or whoever he was had been involved with

that one. Maybe, like some writers, these guys lived their stories. In any case, Bud had no interest in helping them, as he felt that such people were good at using the Hollywood mystique to exploit people like Millie, offering them peanuts to help with productions that would make them millions.

He wasn't the only one here who felt that way, and he knew such shenanigans were generally held in low esteem by the working folks of small towns like Green River—until, like Millie, they were offered money, that is.

He grimaced, hoping Howie would stay clear of it all.

Bud was sitting at his desk, having just put Millie's painting into the evidence safe, when he noticed a giant tumbleweed rolling right down the middle of the street. That generally wasn't that unusual for Green River, except this time the wind wasn't blowing.

He sat there and watched it roll right past the big plate glass window of the Sheriff's Office, then on out of sight. Soon, he saw a truck following with a big fan attached to it, which was what was powering the tumbleweed. Behind that was a film crew in a truck with a big camera, and behind that was an assortment of film people, followed by some followers-on, including Howie, keeping up the rear in the patrol car.

Bud was irritated. Howie was supposed to be out keeping an eye on a small diversion dam that flanked the Green River and brought water in for the area's farmers, as well as the town's lawns. The dam looked like it might soon be topped by the floodwaters, which would mean some flooding along that part of the river, mostly in newly-planted melon fields.

He now forgot about Howie and thought of Krider's melon farm. It was right smack in that area. He wondered if the prof had closed on the property yet. He would call him.

Krider answered, "Hello, Sheriff. How's life treating you?"

"Good, except I'm worried about your new melon farm getting flooded out, Prof. Have you already closed the deal?"

"This morning, first thing. It's now mine, although the fellow who owned it has a couple of weeks still. I wanted him around for a bit to show me the ropes, and he agreed."

"Are you aware that the diversion dam is close to being flooded out?"

Krider paused. "No, I wasn't."

"I had Howie out there keeping a watch on it, but he's found himself another assignment in the meantime. I have to run to the post office, then I'm going on out there."

"Why don't I meet you at the farm, Bud. Then maybe I can ride with you. I'm not even sure where the dam is."

B ud and Krider sat on an old cottonwood log, watching the river slowly eat away at the dam. Bud had been aware that the mountains up in the northeast part of the state had received record snowfall, but he hadn't worried about it too much until now.

They'd had a cool spring, and now that warm weather had arrived everything was melting at once. And apparently the Yampa River, over in Colorado, was also getting full, which would add to the Green River's load.

Bud had been talking with the sheriff up near Jenson, another small town along the Green up north, and they were already having record floods. And it was heading this way.

"What will you do if it floods, Prof?" Bud asked.

"What can I do? Hopefully it won't leave too much junk behind. I'll just have to clean it up. We'll replant, as we'll still have time. We'll have to put down new weed mesh. But it won't be the end of the world. The house and outbuildings are on high ground. Say, Bud, you thought much about coming to work for me?"

"Would you still have work if it floods?"

"I think I would have even more work than usual."

"I talked to Wilma Jean and she says I should go for it, that chances like this don't come around very often. I'd like to do it, Prof, but I have to solve this Joe Swasey case first. I'd also like to give them plenty of notice so they can find someone else."

"What about Howie?"

"I've been giving that a lot of thought. It would make them miss me, I think, if he were sheriff."

"They're going to miss you, anyway, Bud. Anything new about the case?"

"Not really."

"It's turning into a tough case because there's no longer a body," Krider said.

"I know. And I think there might be a reason for that. I've been thinking about what you said about those who have the most to lose. I need to solve this fast, because my main suspect is leaving town."

Krider sat silent. He knew he couldn't ask, but he could speculate.

"I bet that would be Doc Richardson."

"Yup," Bud replied. "You're a good detective, Prof."

"Be careful, Sheriff," Krider replied. "Things aren't always what they seem."

30

Bud sat in his office, but his feet weren't up on his desk, as they usually were. He was being polite because he had company.

"Sheriff, we'd really like to get your Bigfoot story. We heard you've seen one, and for a man in your position to talk about this, well, it would give our case a lot more legitimacy."

The man in the white cowboy hat with the nice tan was practically begging Bud to talk. Howie sat behind his desk looking exasperated, trying not to look at Bud.

"Just what exactly is your case?" Bud asked, thinking the guy's tan somehow didn't look at all like Old Man Green's and the guys he knew who worked outside all the time.

"We think Bigfoot exists, and so far, we've interviewed three people on film talking about encounters right here in Emery County. One guy, who lives over in Orangeville, has seen them seven times. He claims they've even come to visit his house. Mostly they're up on the Wasatch Plateau, he says, and the San Rafael Swell really isn't that far from the Wasatch."

"I thought the Wasatch was up by Salt Lake," Howie commented.

Bud replied, "You're right, Deputy, the Wasatch Mountains, but the Wasatch Plateau is different. It's over between Emery and Salina, that country."

"Right," said the TV director, who had introduced himself earlier as Jacob Samuelson. Bud had thought it was a good name for a director, even if it didn't go with the Stetson. It sounded very New Yorker or Californian. Around here, everyone was named Joe, Hank, Charlie, LaVar, or even Bud—unless you were a woman, of course.

"What I saw wasn't a Bigfoot," Bud added. "And I'm worried you boys are gonna stir up a hornet's nest. We have only myself and my deputy here working law enforcement. We're a big county, but one with few people. If you guys bring a bunch of Bigfoot hunters in here, we're going to send you the bill for rescuing them and dealing with their nonsense. I can't say I'm real happy to have you here, not in the context of what you're doing, anyway. How about a nice special on rafting the Green? You would get my full cooperation on something like that."

"People like mystery and drama," Jacob answered. "And you guys seem to have plenty of it here, especially for such a backwater little burg. But, I guess if you don't want some extra cash, Sheriff, there are others who do."

Bud was irritated at Jacob's demeaning of his little town, even though he had to agree it was pretty much out in the sticks and occasionally reminded him of an open-air lunatic asylum. But what made him mad was the attempt to bribe him, and he said so, whereupon the director stood and left, hat in hand, or rather, white hat in hand.

"Boy, Sheriff, you sure didn't waste words on that guy, did you?" Howie said. He was obviously disappointed, but smart enough to know when thin ice was present. He added, "I wish I'd seen one so I could make some extra cash."

Bud answered, "Who's to say you didn't? You could make up a good story, and they wouldn't know the difference."

"That would be dishonest," Howie countered.

"Well, you wouldn't be the first one."

"Are you saying people who claim they've seen Bigfoot are liars?"

"Some are, yes. Others, I think it was just a case of misidentification. It was a bear or a bush or any number of things. The human mind tries to recognize patterns in things-—it's how our species has survived for so long. If I see something in the bushes, I'm more likely to survive if I think it's a tiger and it isn't, than if I think it's nothing and it turns out to be a tiger. Our brains are programmed to make things into recognizable patterns, whether they're really something or not."

"So I take it you don't believe in Bigfoot."

"Howie, I'm Sheriff of Emery County. I'm responsible for 4,462 square miles of land that has a population of under 10,000 people. If I believed in Bigfoot, I'd be afraid to ever set foot in the backcountry, and that means I wouldn't be doing much of a job, because most of the county is backcountry."

Howie was impressed. He'd have to remember those statistics in case he ever was sheriff. He wrote them down on his desk pad.

~

Bud was sitting in the Chow Down, having a chicken-fried steak and reading the latest from the crime lab up in Salt Lake. He wondered what the bill for all this lab work would be, even though the state paid it.

It was about Joe Swasey's boot, and the results said it had been chewed by a member of the canid family. They'd done DNA tests on the saliva. There was also definitely no blood.

Bud already knew that coyotes had chewed it all up, but he had to be sure. If it had come back as an unknown member of a primate species or some such thing he would have to change course on the case, and his rudder wasn't working that well.

Bud knew that coyotes never kill people, and if the boot had been chewed by coyotes, it was likely that the body had, too, and that meant Joe had died of something else and then been chewed up. It was likely that the coyotes had pulled his boot off in the process.

He hesitated, then called Doc Richardson's office. The Doc was busy, as usual, but would call Bud back. The receptionist then added that it was the doctor's last day and that Bud should make arrangements to have his medical records sent to another doctor.

Bud politely told her he wasn't a patient, but thanks anyway, and did she know where the doctor was going? She said somewhere in Colorado, and the conversation ended as she got another call.

Bud's cell phone rang in a few minutes, and it was the doc. He either hadn't been very busy or was really on it today.

"Doc, Joe was chewed up by coyotes. I just got the lab results back." Bud looked around the cafe to make sure no one could overhear him.

"What lab results?"

"We found one of his boots and I sent it in. DNA test said canids, coyotes."

"But Bud, coyotes don't kill people."

"I know, Doc. Something else killed him."

There was a long pause. Finally, Doc said, quietly, "What do you want me to do, Sheriff?"

Bud was taken aback. "I don't know. I'm just looking for answers. I know someone killed him. Are you sure you didn't see anything else, some clue?"

"Bud, I was really tired that day. Joanne and I had been fighting, and she told me she was leaving me. I probably could have done a better job, I realize that now. I was questioning my life, everything about it, especially why I would want to be coroner. It's an elected position, and I think I was taken in by the popularity, as well as wanting to help. But so far, all my wanting to help has just complicated my life. Plus, I don't really enjoy dealing with dead people, as the live ones are bad enough."

He paused. "I'm looking forward to leaving and starting over. One more day here, then I'm gone. All I can say right now is this—I wish I'd never met Millie Mortenson."

With that, he hung up the phone.

31

Bud was back out at the diversion dam, checking it out. It didn't look any better than before, maybe a bit worse. He had called up to Jensen, and things there were getting very serious. The Green was well over its banks, and they were evacuating nearby livestock and property.

He got on the phone with the mayor, who had been staying in touch with the people up at Flaming Gorge Dam, which sat upriver a number of miles, up above Jensen near the Colorado state line. The Bureau of Reclamation had been releasing water from the dam as fast as they possibly could, but the flood waters were coming in fast.

If the Green River diversion dam topped over, its loss was a casualty of minor importance in the grand scale of things, as they would be trying to save the town itself. They were anticipating the river to come up several feet above flood level within the next few days, as the weather was forecast to get unseasonably hot. A few melon farms would be sacrificed, but it couldn't be helped. Bud knew Krider's would be one of them.

Bud drove back towards town, then decided to stop at the house. There was something he needed to check out.

He pulled up just as Wilma Jean was leaving.

"Hey, who's this handsome stranger?" she laughed.

Bud wasn't feeling so happy, and he just smiled. Wilma Jean stopped.

"Hon, are you doing OK? You look pretty haggard."

"I'm OK."

"Have you talked to Krider yet about the job?"

"I told him I want it, but I have to solve the Swasey case first."

"Hon," she asked. "Why?"

"It's my job. I'm the sheriff."

"Why not let the next sheriff take over?"

"It's too complicated. Plus, it's become sort of a personal goal. Look, something's not right about it, and I have to figure it out. It's bugging me."

"Well, I can say this, not having a husband any more is kind of bugging me."

Wilma Jean drove off.

Bud went into the house, thinking about Doc and Joanne. They say couples often split up because of money problems. The Doc had no money problems, not that Bud knew of, anyway. If he'd had money problems, why was he giving it away so freely? But then maybe he had money problems because he was giving it away so freely.

But he knew another big reason for splitting up was a lack of communication. He and Wilma Jean were cruising down that highway together, he thought, and it was entirely because they never saw each other. And that was Joe Swasey's fault.

He wondered how he could blame a dead man for anything, opened the door, and Pierre immediately attacked his pant leg. The little dog had been hiding behind the corner, and Hoppie was there right next to him, egging him on, barking his fool head off.

~

Bud was sipping hot coffee and once again going through the photos he'd taken up at Joe's cabin. Something wasn't right. He'd been feeling it before, and that's why he'd gone back to the cabin to spend the night, though the guy in the Bigfoot suit had interrupted that plan.

He studied the photo taken from the foot of the cot, the one where the body was skewed a bit. He just couldn't figure it out. The found boot had to be Joe's, as there was one just like it on the other foot.

He got up and refilled his cup, sitting back down and rubbing the bridge of his nose. Something was off. He'd met Joe at the Ghost Rock Cafe a few times, though he never really talked to him, and he seemed like a nice enough guy, not someone you would guess to be a hermit, other than his appearance, anyway. He was a big guy, tall with broad shoulders, and he looked a little scruffy, but he seemed congenial enough and fairly intelligent.

Then it hit Bud. He knew what was wrong.

He thought of the dream he'd had where Joe was saying "I may not be dead, but get the doc." Bud had thought the dream was telling him to go for the doctor, as Joe needed medical help, but maybe that's not what Joe had been saying at all.

Bud's subconscious had picked something up, and that's why Bud kept having this nagging feeling.

Maybe Joe had been telling Bud to get the doc, as in arrest him, but why would Joe say he wasn't even dead, and why would Bud reply that Joe wasn't even injured? It was a puzzle, just like Old Man Green's missing steers.

It was just a dream, Bud told himself, but he knew his intuition was trying to tell him something. And in spite of thinking he'd maybe figured out the dream, that nagging feeling still hadn't gone away. Something was still off.

Bud now zoomed in on the photo. He studied the cot a bit, trying to get a feel for its size. Probably just a standard camping cot, not an oversized one, and they were probably all the same length. Because the body was skewed a bit, it was hard to tell. Bud looked and thought and rubbed his nose until he finally decided he was getting the picture.

That's what had been bothering him all along, and now he knew he had finally truly figured it out. It's why he had gone back to the cabin and waited. He knew deep inside that someone else would show up, and he had no doubt about who that someone was.

Shortly thereafter, Bud sat in a booth at the Willows, alone. Soon, a pretty woman with black eyes and long black hair tied in a ponytail sat down across from him.

"Maria, sorry to intrude on your working time, but I need your help."

"Es no problema, Sheriff," she replied. "Es OK."

"Can you translate this for me?" Bud handed her a printout of an email he'd just received. It was from someone in Aguescalientes, Mexico. It had arrived on his computer yesterday, but he'd been putting off dealing with it.

"Si, bien."

She sat and read for a moment, then said, "Es very sad. Es una familia de Mexico, sus padre, he no go alla, es missing. Es un sheepherder aqui, here in Los Estados Unidos, Green River, y no go home. Es missing por muchas dias ahora. Seven days, he missing, no go home to Aguescalientes like he says. La familia es muy worried."

"What a shame. I feel for them," Bud answered. "OK, Maria, muchas gracias. Thanks very much."

He handed her a ten dollar bill, which she didn't want to take, but finally relented.

She went back into the kitchen while Bud sat for a moment, not sure what to do next. Finally, he stood and went out the door, slowly getting into his old red Bronco.

32

Bud pulled into the Ghost Rock Cafe, noting the Utah School of Mines bus was gone. He parked next to the black stretch Rover, kind of miffed that it was there, because that meant one thing—they were still doing the Bigfoot special. No, it meant two things—his back booth would also be taken.

As he entered, Millie jumped up, seeing him.

"Bud! You're here! Boy, do I have some news for you!"

Just then, Larry walked through the door behind him. He was wearing a bright fluorescent green ball cap with the words *Do the Melon Mash, Green River Melon Days.*

Millie said, "Larry! You survived another dy-no-mite haul. Sit down, guys, I have some news."

They sat down in the front booth. Bud noticed there were no geology students around, just an older couple at the bar, drinking milkshakes. They looked like tourists, from the looks of their clothes, or maybe someone from Price, where there were nice clothing stores.

"I just sold the cafe," Millie announced, sitting by Larry and putting her arm around him and hugging him. "Can you believe it?"

Larry was speechless, but Bud said, "I didn't know it was for sale, Millie."

Larry now recovered, saying, "I didn't either, Mill. Who bought it?"

"That gentleman over there in the back booth," She pointed at the same guy who had been in Bud's office, Jacob Samuelson.

"Holy crap, Millie," Bud said, "You sold out to Hollywood?"

Millie acted insulted. "Sold out? What do you mean by that?"

Bud replied, "What I mean, Millie, is that now we get to be stuck with these guys while you lay around on some tropical beach with all your cash. But don't get me wrong, I'm very happy for you, though I'll miss you. Where are you going?"

Millie said, still miffed, "Look, Bud, that guy over there isn't going to be here any more than you or I will be. He's buying it for a movie set. He loves this run-down junky place and wants to use it in a series he's going to do."

"A series?" Bud tried not to groan out loud.

"Yeah, about Bigfoot. It's going to have the motel as the place where everyone always gathers and such, sort of the Bigfoot head-quarters. He's going to keep the name, the Ghost Rock Cafe. He's also talking about putting in a Bigfoot museum for tourists."

Larry responded, "And you say he's not going to be here? Looks to me like he's moving in. So, Mill, looks like you owe me." He was now smiling.

"For what?"

"If I'd been doing my job, you know, maintaining the place, putting in daisy flower beds and painting it sunburst yellow and all that, they wouldn't have wanted it."

"Good point" Millie said, then added quietly. "But I got a fortune for it—way, way more than it's worth. My attorney from Price just wrote up the papers and they just transferred a bunch of money for a deposit—heck, the deposit alone is about what the place is worth. My attorney even said he couldn't believe what I'm getting. We'll close in one week."

"I think they may have bought a bit more than they bargained for," Larry said.

"What?" Millie asked.

"They're going to have some real good Bigfoot stories."

Millie got quiet. "I never thought of that." She then added, "And Bud, to answer your question, I'm going to Colorado. I want to live next to an alfalfa field on the edge of some little town in a cozy bungalow like you and Wilma Jean have. I'm sick of the desert—and being scared to death at night. I'll miss my ravens, but not the buzzards."

She smiled, nodding towards the back booth.

Later, Bud and Larry were enjoying hot apple pie a la mode when Professor Cole walked in.

"Come join, us, Prof." Bud motioned to the seat next to him.

The prof sat down. He was wearing a baseball cap that read, *Burgess Shale, Yoho Nat'l Park* on it. Larry must be rubbing off on him, Bud thought.

"I'm tired. I can't keep up with these kids any more. They wear me out," Professor Cole moaned.

"Where is everyone?" Larry asked.

"In the motel. We just got back from a little field trip down to the Green River Geyser, down your way, Bud."

The geyser was a rare cold-water geyser, powered by pressure instead of by heat, like most geysers. It was the result of an oil exploration company drilling test holes and hitting carbon dioxide, right next to the river. It was unpredictable, erupting only every 12 hours or so.

"That's a fun trip. I haven't been out there for awhile. Did it erupt?"

"We got lucky. That darn thing must shoot up 60 feet."

Larry asked, "Did you notice the little mud pots next to it, how they get going crazy before it erupts? They sound like water boiling, even though they're cold."

"I did notice that," the prof answered. "The travertine around the geyser is really beautiful. And something else, did you ever notice that band of calcite up in the cliffs just a bit before you get to the geyser? About four feet thick. Really exceptional."

Just then, several students came in, and Professor Cole stood to go, adding, "Hey, excuse me. I need to see what the plan is for dinner. We're talking about doing a big bonfire over behind the motel. Millie's going to provide hot dogs and all that. You guys come join us in a couple of hours. It's the end of our field class. We're leaving tomorrow and it's a tradition to have a big celebration. These kids are all geologists now."

With that, Professor Cole left, joining the students.

"You hanging around for that?" Larry asked.

"I think I might," Bud answered. He was a bit perturbed to know they were leaving. It seemed the Swell had become a more welcoming place with the kids around.

"I'm gonna go take a shower, then I'll see you back at the fire ring later." Larry got up and left.

Bud sat there for a bit, wondering where Roger was. He was also thinking of Doc Richardson, wondering where he'd be going after leaving Price, which would be tomorrow. He decided to call Wilma Jean.

"Hi, Hon," she answered. "I know, you're calling to tell me you're not coming home tonight."

"I dunno. I miss you. I just want to tell you I love you."

Wilma Jean was silent for a bit, then said, "Is everything OK?"

"Maybe, I dunno. Look, Wilma Jean, I'm up at the Ghost Rock Cafe. Millie just sold it. Things are winding down here—she's leaving in a week. I'm running out of time to solve this case, and I think I'm onto something. I just need a little more time. But whatever happens, hon, I love you, I just want you to know that."

"What do you mean, whatever happens? Are you in some kind of danger?"

"No, no, I didn't mean to worry you at all. I'm just needing to be up here one more night, then I think I may be able to wrap it all up. You take good care of the kids. I'll see you tomorrow."

"OK, hon. Be careful, and I love you, too."

Bud's next call was to Howie.

"Howie, Bud here. How's things going over at the river?"

"OK, I guess."

"Have you been over to check the dam?"

"Not lately, Sheriff."

"When was the last time you were over there?"

"I dunno. I guess it was just before the movie guys asked me to provide them with a police escort for the tumbleweed scene."

"That was a long time ago. Has the mayor called?"

"No." Howie was wishing he could get back to his story in *True Crime* before he forgot what the plot was, as it was getting complicated.

"OK. Anything else going on?"

"Not really. I had to go help a couple of tourists break into their car. They'd locked themselves out."

"Are you sure it was their car?" Bud joked.

Howie got all serious. "Sheriff, I never even thought of that. How would I know?"

Bud said, "Howie, I wouldn't worry about it too much. Usually thieves aren't able to find cars with the keys locked in them, and they definitely don't call the sheriff's office to help them break in."

Now Howie was worried. "But seriously, how would I know? I mean, could I be charged with aiding and abetting?"

"No, Howie, not a chance. Don't worry about it."

"OK, Sheriff, that's a relief. I guess next time I'll ask them for ID. Oh, and you got a letter today from some lab in Washington, D.C."

Bud was miffed at Howie again. This was what he'd been waiting for, and Howie had almost forgotten to tell him, and it was critical information for the Swasey case.

"Howie, open it and read it to me."

He could hear paper crinkling, then, "It says the use of Nuclear and Mini Filer DNA extraction processes are valuable for court of law case proceedings and can offer the potential for evaluating for the presence of heavy metals including mercury, lead, and many others."

Bud interrupted. "Howie, just read the specifics for what the lab sent. I don't need to know the general stuff."

"OK. It basically says that the cremains sent had a moderate but non-lethal percentage of cyanide in them."

Bud thought for a bit. "OK, Howie, that's all I need to know. Thanks."

He hung up before Howie could start grilling him. The ashes had cyanide in them, which confirmed what he'd thought ever since he found that boot and studied the photo of the body on the cot. He felt one-hundred percent sure that he knew who the murderer was now, and he felt relaxed. He could solve this case.

If he could arrest the person he thought had done it and get a DNA sample, he knew it would match that on the hamburger. That might make his case in court, as he realized the evidence he had so far was pretty much circumstantial.

Bud now called Krider.

"You been over to the dam lately?"

"I have, Bud, and it looks real bad. I've been over there helping the farmer move equipment. I sure wish you were here."

"I can't tell you how bad I wish that, too, Prof." Bud said. "I'm up at the Ghost Rock, and it looks like it's gonna be another long night, but I hope to be down there tomorrow and help however I can."

"Making any progress?"

"I think so. I'll know after tonight."

"OK, Bud. Be safe."

"Thanks."

33

The bonfire crackled and roared, throwing sparks into the air. Bud and Larry and Millie sat together on a big log, watching the geology students do a wild dance in a circle around the fire, chanting something that sounded like:

Eons, eras, periods, and epochs,
Orogenies, transgressions, and big regressions, too.
Rock hammers, altimeters, mass wasting and rock cycles,
Tectonic plates, subduction zones, Creationists with no clue.

Bud shook his head. He couldn't believe it. It seemed like the end of field school was some form of pagan ritual, and Professor Cole was right out there with them, dancing around and chanting.

Debris flows and isotopes, laccoliths and obtuse slopes,
Anticlines and monoclines and fossiliferous stew.
Trilobites and biotites, dips and slopes and dolomites,
Stromatolites and halites, and gastrolithic glue.
Ai yay, ai yay, we're scientists now, ai yay,
Ai yay, ai yay, geology or the highway,

Ai yay, ai yay, pass the beer my way,
We'll save your ass for another day,
Geologists love their brew.

"They're getting drunker than skunks," Millie laughed. "Good thing they're the only ones staying in the motel."

"Speaking of which, I'm turning in," Larry announced. "I drove all the way from Albuquerque and I'm tired. I could sleep though anything. G'night, all."

"Me, too, it's past my bedtime," Millie said. She and Larry left Bud sitting on the log, Millie heading over to her little trailer and Larry to the motel.

Bud sat there for awhile, wondering what it would've been like if he'd gone to college. He always enjoyed geology, what little he knew, and he loved rock hounding.

But he hadn't, he'd become sheriff instead, and he had work to do. He slipped quietly away, getting into his Bronco, and headed for Swasey's cabin.

By the time he got to his parking spot hidden in the juniper grove, he was already having second thoughts. Dang it, maybe Wilma Jean was right. Why not just announce he was leaving and let the new sheriff handle this?

He could debrief him on everything, get him up to speed, and go be a melon farmer. It seemed so peaceful, and he'd be home every night with his family. He wondered if Hoppie and Pierre were snuggled down under the blankets with Wilma Jean, and he wished he was there with them.

There was a time when Bud would have relished the thought of sitting out on a night like this, surrounded by the peace and quiet under a blanket of stars. He used to camp a lot, sometimes alone, and sometimes Wilma Jean would come with him, but they'd both gotten so busy they'd just let it eventually go by the wayside.

But now Bud must be getting older, because he craved the security of the bungalow and its big porch under the cottonwoods, the nice grassy lawn and old barn.

He got out of the Bronco and leaned against it for a bit, listening to the crickets and other night sounds. He wasn't relishing what he was about to do.

If his hunch was right, the next step would be to get the judge over at the courthouse in Castle Dale to issue an arrest warrant. He didn't plan on taking any action at all tonight, even if his suspicions were correct, he would just observe and confirm his theory as to who the murderer was. But he knew it could be dangerous business, and he wasn't in any hurry to proceed.

Now he started thinking about what he'd seen the last time he stood here in the dark, and he started wondering if maybe Larry wasn't right, that there was a real live Bigfoot out here, as well as someone in a suit.

What if it had been a real Bigfoot that night over in Hondu Country? Bud had written it off to imagination, or maybe the dirt bikers had been playing tricks on them.

He didn't go much for superstition, partly because he was too pragmatic, but also because he knew it would make his job even harder. He couldn't afford to go there.

He was procrastinating, and he knew it. He pulled his jacket tight around him, checked his gun, grabbed his big police flashlight, and quietly walked towards the cabin in the dark. He had no intention of anyone seeing him.

He walked down the road for a bit, then veered over to the big pinion tree he'd sat under the last time. Then he changed his mind. He knew exactly where to go now. He hadn't been so sure last time.

He slowly and carefully made his way around the back of the cabin and over to the cliffs, then around on the other side of the alcove, hiding in the thick scrub oak where he could see but not be seen. He settled down onto the dried leaves and tried to get comfortable. It could be a long night.

He couldn't help but think of Krider's melon farm again. He wondered if it would be flooded. He thought about spending all day out there, in the quiet and big cottonwoods, managing the place, farming it, and in some ways it would be better than owning it, as he wouldn't have to come up with the cash to pay for everything.

Then he started wondering if it would be the right thing to do. Police work could get pretty routine, but it usually was never boring. What if he got bored out on the farm and regretted quitting?

But he'd been in law enforcement for over five years now, and it seemed every year he and Wilma Jean were going their own ways more and more. He was tired of that and wanted to be home more, to do things with her. He missed her. And even if he were really busy during the spring and summer, they'd have winters together when things were slow on the farm. He could even help her out some at the bowling alley and cafe.

The night wore on, and Bud got sleepy. He had anticipated this and brought a little can of some kind of caffeinated drink with him. It was called *MegaWake* and claimed to keep one awake for the whole night.

He hadn't bothered to see what was in it, because he didn't want to know. He just wanted to stay awake. Larry had told him about it. Apparently it was popular with truck drivers.

Bud reached into his jacket pocket and pulled it out, quietly popping the can open. He sat sipping it when he noticed movement. Something was coming up from the canyon.

He quickly finished the drink and put his hand on his gun. There wasn't a moon out tonight, and it was black as tar. This made the stars hang in the sky like you could reach out and touch them, but it sure didn't make for good spying.

Now, whoever or whatever it was, it was coming up to the alcove. Bud wasn't initially sure that it wasn't an animal or something, but he immediately knew it was human when he saw a little penlight go on. It flashed around in the holly bushes a bit as whoever it was pushed their way into the alcove.

He could tell they were in the alcove by the way the light disappeared and then occasionally flashed inside.

He sat in silence. He wasn't sure what to do at this point. He had hoped the visibility would be a little better and he could see who it was, but he couldn't see a thing. He just sat there.

But now he could hear a vehicle in the distance. It looked to be a repeat of last time he was here, as someone was coming down the road. He wondered if it would be Professor Cole and Jimmy again.

He was back at an angle behind the cliffs where he couldn't see the cabin, but he heard the vehicle stop and two car doors close. Whoever it was, there were two of them.

Bud toyed with the idea of sneaking over there, but he had to find out who had gone into the alcove, as it was crucial to confirming his hunch and to solving the murder, so he waited.

Now whoever was in the alcove had apparently also heard the vehicle, for they were coming back out. He still couldn't make anything out, as they pushed back through the holly bushes, penlight still on. Then the light went out, and he could hear them walk by, only a few feet from him, towards the cabin. He thought for a moment they would walk right into him, but they didn't, passing quietly.

Bud sat in the bushes, wondering what to do. If he got up and followed, he might give himself away. But he needed to do something, just sitting and hoping he could identify anyone in this blackness wasn't getting him anywhere.

Now he could hear a voice coming from the cabin. It was a woman, and she was talking loud. He strained to hear and finally made it out.

It was Millie.

34

Bud slipped out of the scrub oak and silently made his way over to the cabin, but by a different route than that of the stranger in the night.

He went over towards the cabin's front and then to the pinion tree where he'd sat the last time he'd been out here spying, climbing into its protective branches. It was a familiar place. He could barely make out the outline of a vehicle sitting near the cabin, but nothing more.

Millie was having an argument with someone, and she was yelling, angry. He could see a dim light in the cabin, like a lantern.

Now he could hear another voice, and he strained to make out who it was. Soon, the door of the cabin opened. Millie came out, and she was crying.

Now, Bud could make out what was being said, and he could also make out who was talking. It was Doc Richardson!

"Millie, I gave you that money so you could get out of here, that's why. It wasn't a payoff of any such kind. Why I even told you it was me is beyond me. Who in the hellsbells do you think I am, anyway?"

Bud had never heard Doc use this tone of voice, as he'd always been quiet and soft spoken.

Millie replied, "Then why are you leaving, just like that? You have no intention of coming back here, you're just going to leave me here to rot. Not that I would be here, anyway."

The doc seemed surprised. "Why not? Where would you be?"

"I sold the cafe. I'm history."

"No way. Sold the cafe?"

"I'm out of here in one week. Maybe less."

"My God, Millie, that changes everything."

"How so?"

Bud strained to hear her answer, but the conversation continued without him, because he was suddenly knocked cold by something that felt a bit like a big stick, or so he thought, just before slumping down along the pinion's trunk and losing consciousness.

When Bud woke, he had no idea where he was. It was pitch black, and all he knew was that his head hurt, as well as his right arm. He was going to have to tell Larry that the *MegaWake* hadn't worked too well.

He pulled his arm out from where he'd been lying on it and shook it a bit. It had gone to sleep. It was his gun hand, too, he noted with concern.

He did a quick assessment to see how seriously he was hurt, only to find he was OK, other than his head hurting. Why someone would whack him on the head, he had no idea. He soon recalled where he was and why.

The vehicle, which he now knew was probably Doc's Land Rover, was gone, as well as Doc and Millie. He sat there, not knowing what to do.

Just like the last time he'd tried doing a stakeout, it had failed, though this time it had been a tad more personal. He rubbed his head.

Bud later revisited what he did next and the logic behind it and always wondered why. He had to write it off to shock from a concussion, as there was certainly no logical explanation for being so careless with one's own life.

Wilma Jean later told him it was the Irish in him, and he was just plain angry.

He stood up and walked to his Bronco, making no effort to be quiet. He then got in and started it and drove back down to the cabin, leaving the lights shining in the door while he got out and searched the interior.

No one was there, and he saw nothing new. The crime tape appeared to have blown away. He then got back into the Bronco and drove it as far towards the alcove as he could and then got out, leaving the engine running and the lights shining towards the cliffs.

He turned on his police flashlight and walked towards the alcove, pushing his way in through the holly, unafraid. No one was there. There was an old sleeping bag on the ground and a metal camp chair.

He had pushed his way back out through the holly and was turning to leave when he saw something standing on the rim of Eagle Canyon. It was huge, and its eyes glowed red.

Bud didn't even pause, he just pulled out his gun.

The creature screamed, and it made Bud's blood run cold. It started coming at him.

The sound of Bud's gunfire echoed off the cliffs, back and forth for quite some time, far into the distance.

Bud hadn't aimed to kill or even injure it, rather he had purposely aimed a bit to the side. He wanted to scare it, that was all.

It stopped and stood there.

Bud started talking to it, slow and resolute, unafraid.

"I know who you really are, and I'm coming up here tomorrow afternoon with an arrest warrant. You can be waiting in the cabin and come peacefully, or you can come out as a dead body. It's your choice. If I have to, I'll hunt you down until one of us is dead, and it won't be me."

He continued, "If you come out on your own volition, you'll get off with manslaughter charges, since I don't believe it was a premeditated murder. Since it's your first offense, you'll probably only get a few years in prison, then you can get on with your life again, start over, make of it what you want."

Bud was playing his ace in the hole. He had no confirmation that the man in the suit was who he thought it was, and he didn't want to arrest him until he had convinced the judge he had a case. He was bluffing. And he hoped to heck the man in the suit wasn't armed.

Then the thought flashed through his head that maybe it really was a Bigfoot, and how foolish he would feel for trying to talk a Bigfoot into letting him arrest it.

He saw the humor in it, even while standing there in the night with the creature's eyes glowing at him, and he couldn't help but smile. He had no fear. Something had changed in him. He knew this was the last case he would ever take on, then he was going to be a melon farmer.

Bud then added, with compassion in his voice, "I know what happened, and I'll personally make sure you get a good attorney, the best. But you have to man up to what you did, it was wrong."

The creature stood there, looking at Bud, its eyes glowing in the black night, then turned and disappeared back down into the black depths of Eagle Canyon, just as Bud passed out again.

35

Bud was now awake, having no idea how long he'd been out this time. He made it back to his Bronco, still feeling woozy.

He was halfway back to the Ghost Rock Cafe when he saw Doc's Rover coming up the road towards the cabin. Bud was surprised. He stopped and waited for Doc to pull up next to him.

"What the heck, Sheriff, are you OK? We heard a gunshot."

Now Bud could see that Roger and Professor Cole were also in the Land Rover. He tried to answer, but couldn't. He'd been running on sheer adrenaline, but now things were again catching up to him.

He opened his mouth to talk and everything went red, just like the creature's eyes, and he promptly passed out yet again, slumping down into the seat, popping the clutch and killing the engine.

Roger jumped out and put on the Bronco's emergency brake, and Doc Richardson and the professor were soon there, helping get Bud out of the vehicle.

They laid him on the ground, and the doc did a quick assessment, quickly finding the head wound, which was slowly oozing blood. He got out his emergency kit, and soon Bud was in the back of the Rover with Doc at his side and Roger driving, while Professor Cole drove the Bronco, weaving a bit.

They pulled into the motel and unloaded Bud in Roger's motel room, placing him onto the bed. There, Doc tried to do what he could, cleaning the wound. Millie was soon there, looking pale and scared.

Doc was pretty sure it wasn't major, but he really wished Bud would wake up. If he didn't before long, he would have to take him down to the hospital in Price.

As if he'd heard Doc talking, Bud finally awakened.

They decided Bud should spend the night at Millie's again, so they slowly walked him over there and tucked him into her bed. He kept telling them to call Wilma Jean, and they said they already had.

That's all Bud remembered before he fell into a deep sleep, one with no dreams, not even of Krider's melon farm.

Doc Richardson's big Land Rover sat in front of Millie's trailer, as he wanted to be close in case Bud took a turn for the worse, though he didn't think he would, it looking like a somewhat moderate concussion.

He would drive Bud down to the hospital in the morning to get x-rays if he weren't better, but for now, Bud needed rest.

~

Bud woke and once again had no idea where he was. This was getting to be a regular thing, he thought. Maybe he needed to start carrying a GPS. It was dark, his head hurt, and he was hungry.

"Doc! Doc! He's waking up!"

Bud kind of recognized the voice, but not really. He could see that the door was open just enough to show the outline of the door jamb, but he still couldn't figure out where he was. He did finally determine that someone was sitting by his bed.

Now the door opened and light streamed in.

He was in Millie's bedroom again. How the heck did he get here? Maybe the whole thing had been a dream and he was still here from the night they'd found Millie. He sat up.

"Sit still, Bud, don't move around until I can examine you."

It was Doc Richardson.

"Is he going to be OK?"

There was that voice again. At first he thought it was Millie, but now he knew it wasn't. Now someone was kissing his forehead.

It was Wilma Jean!

Bud slipped back down into bed. All would be well. Wilma Jean was here.

R oger walked over to Millie's trailer, having just had breakfast at the cafe. He was a bit bleary eyed, as he and Professor Cole had spent half the night going over Joe Swasey's rock collection. He knew he'd had orders to not show it to the prof, but he couldn't hide a room full of rocks when they'd brought Bud into his room last night. He had also decided to show the prof the uranium samples behind the motel.

They ended up having the geology students load the rocks into the bus. Roger would keep what he wanted and donate the rest to the School of Mines.

He knocked on Millie's door, and she answered.

"Come in, Rog. You look tired."

"I am. I drank too much and stayed up all night, a bad combination. How's Bud?"

"I think he's gonna be OK. The doc is in there with him and his wife. She came up last night. You kids set to leave?"

"Yeah, just about. Millie, it's been quite an experience. They say field camp is the highlight of your geology education, but I don't think they meant like this. I'm hating to go, though I'm looking forward to seeing my wife."

"I didn't know you were married! What does she do?"

"She's in law enforcement for the Park Service. We met when I was working at Canyonlands National Park as an archaeologist. She's about to have our first baby."

"Gosh," Millie replied. "I sure meet some interesting people up here. I'm gonna miss this place. Good luck with the newborn and congratulations. But I gotta get back to the cafe, and I need to feed my birds. Go on in."

Roger entered the dark room, greeting Doc Richardson and Wilma Jean. It was the first time he'd met Bud's wife.

"How is he?" he asked.

"I think he's gonna be OK," Doc answered.

"Hey, Bud, how you feeling?" Roger asked.

Bud answered. "Better than I did last night, I guess. Those power drinks sure can do a number on you."

Roger laughed. "Bud, I've come to say goodbye. We're all heading out shortly, assuming Professor Cole can get rid of his hangover enough to drive."

Bud now sat up and tried to get out of bed. Wilma Jean and the Doc both protested, but he said, "I gotta get up now. I have things to do, and I need to talk to Roger."

"We'll leave you alone to talk," Doc said. He and Wilma Jean left the room.

"Rog, you're leaving?" Bud asked.

"I have to go with them, Bud, I don't have any way to get home otherwise, but I wish I could stay and help you with the case. Are you any closer to solving it after last night?"

"I am, Rog, and I need you to help me this afternoon. I'm going to make an arrest. I need to call the judge first, but I don't feel up to doing it alone."

"How about asking Doc Richardson?"

"I don't think that would work too well."

"How about Larry?"

"He's not real good in a crisis, he starts crying."

"Jeez, Bud I wish I could stay."

"I can get you back home. It might be dangerous, but I really don't think it will."

"No, Bud, I'm not worried about that. It's just that my wife really wants me to come home. She's pregnant and about to have the baby any minute. It's our first. I haven't seen her for six weeks."

"Well, Rog, that's different. Family always takes precedence." He hoped Wilma Jean wasn't listening in. "Don't you worry, I'll find someone. I'll call my deputy, it's actually his job, not yours."

"It's been great knowing you, Bud."

"You too, Rog. Come down sometime and bring the family. I mean that. You can always find me on Krider's melon farm."

"How so?"

"I'm quitting the sheriff position. Giving my notice tomorrow."

"Wow, sounds great. They'll miss you."

Roger offered his hand to Bud, who, instead of shaking it, pulled him to him and gave him a hug.

"You're my tribe," Bud said. "Now get going and call me later and let me know when you have the kid."

"I will, and be safe," Roger said, stepping out of the room.

Bud slipped out of bed and put on his boots. He'd slept in his clothes again. It was getting to be a habit, he thought. Oh well, it saved getting dressed and undressed.

He needed to make a phone call to the judge over in Castle Dale, then he wanted to get something to eat.

He was doing this all backwards, he knew. He should've just arrested the guy last night. He knew other sheriffs did it that way. It was called the bird in the hand method.

But he had to convince the judge he had a case, and maybe convince himself, too. The evidence was kind of inferential, at least until they could make the arrest and match the hamburger DNA. If it did match, that would cinch it. Maybe.

He sat back down and dialed the county courthouse, over in Castle Dale.

36

Bud stood in the kitchen of the Ghost Rock Cafe, watching Millie, who was making a grilled cheese sandwich for a customer.

Wilma Jean had gone back down to Green River after making sure Bud would be OK, and Doc Richardson had gone back to Price. Bud wondered where the doc would go next.

Bud had told Wilma Jean he'd be coming down later, and he was going to talk to the mayor and resign, give him two week's notice if they needed it. He noted that this seemed to make her very happy.

Maybe there was hope for their marriage after all. He knew his injury had proved to him that she still cared, and he knew he cared about her. Not much more to think about there, two people care, and it's all going to work out, he thought.

Millie took the sandwich out to the dining room, then came back in.

"Bud, I'm so glad you're OK," she said. "I had no idea you were out there, and I know you had to have heard what me and Doc were talking about, so let me fill in the details, as you're going to find out anyway."

Bud had no idea what she was talking about, except he vaguely recalled that she and Doc Richardson had been out at the cabin last night, before he got hit on the head.

"Look, Doc gave me the money to help me out, that's all there was to it. I originally thought it was a payoff, he was paying me for...well, because he felt guilty."

"Guilty about what, Millie?"

"Well, it's embarrassing, as he's a married man, but guilty for seeing me, I guess. His wife was cheating on him and had been for years, and he knew it. But he wouldn't leave her because of the kids. He's a good man, Bud."

She continued. "But he would sometimes stop up here on his way to Salina, he would go over there when they needed a doctor at the low-income clinic. He has a good heart. He'd stop here, and one thing led to another. He didn't want anyone to know, so we snuck around a lot. I'd go meet him over by the Ghost Rock."

"We fell in love, but he still wouldn't leave his wife. I finally got tired of the situation and broke it off. He told me he wished he'd never met me. He knew I wanted to leave and had been having problems, so he later sent the money up through you. He probably figured I wouldn't take it if I knew it was from him, and he was right."

"But now that his wife is leaving him, he's a free man. I had told him a lot of times I would never leave the cafe, so he was planning on heading over to Colorado, maybe go into practice with his daughter, who just got out of med school. It was pretty much over with us, as there was no way he could stay in Price, or wanted to, anyway. And Green River's too small to support a practice, so he had to leave if he wanted to make a living. But now that the cafe's sold, I can go wherever he is."

She turned and showed Bud a ring. It was a beautiful diamond.

"He came up yesterday and gave me this. As soon as he gets divorced, we're getting engaged. We're moving over to Colorado, to Palisade, where my son lives, and we're going to get a little house out at the edge of town by the peach orchards. Bud, I can't tell you how happy I am."

Bud didn't have much to say. He couldn't help it, but his mind was on the date he'd made with a murderer that afternoon. And his head still hurt.

"Millie, I'm very happy for you. What's Larry going to do now?"

"He's moving to Elmo, down by Price. He found a little farm to buy. He's like you, he likes farming, but he's going to keep driving truck until he can save enough to buy some equipment. He's going to grow hay."

"Good, I hope I see him once in awhile. But Millie, I need your help, and it's not going to be easy for you. But let me ask you, if someone you cared about had committed a crime, a serious crime, what would you do?"

She thought for a moment.

"If it had anything to do with a bank, I'd say good for them. But if they had harmed someone else, I wouldn't like that."

"But what would you do?" Bud persisted. "Would you turn them in?"

"It would depend on the crime," she answered.

"What if it was murder?"

She didn't hesitate. "I would call the law."

Bud took her arm. "Millie, someone you know and care about has committed murder. I need your help to convict them, because I really don't have enough evidence to win in court. The judge won't issue an arrest warrant, so I need a confession or a witness, and we know this guy's not going to trot down and turn himself in. I need you, because you're the only one I think he would confess to. I need you to talk to him and record it. Will you help me? It could be dangerous."

Millie looked disturbed. "Isn't it illegal to record a conversation?"

"Not if one of the parties involved knows it's being recorded. It's only illegal if nobody knows, like someone hiding in the bushes or something."

"Oh, I didn't know that," she said. Bud could tell she was seriously conflicted, and she looked like she might start crying.

He said, "Millie, it will really be a shock to you, I know it will, so be sure you really will help. You can't change your mind midstream. But I can't do it without you."

She finally said, "That dead man was someone's baby. His momma loved him. His family loved him. Joe was my friend. I can't just stand by and not let justice be served. I don't want to be around anyone who would murder someone, I don't care how much I care about them, it's wrong, dead wrong. Bud, I'll help. Just tell me what questions to ask."

37

Bud and Millie had just left the cafe and headed for the Swasey cabin in the Bronco when Bud's radio crackled.

"Sheriff, you coming down here today?"

"I hope so, Howie. What's up?"

"You know that guy who lives way way down the river and has a fruit farm, what do you call it—an orchard? The skinny guy with the long hair and beard who lives in his old Airstream and has eleven dogs?"

Bud said he did, amazed at the level of information Howie was providing.

"Well, he just came in and said he needed our help."

It looked like the information gusher had just dried up, Bud thought.

"How so?"

"He wants to get his dogs fixed and wants the county to pay for it, but he wouldn't tell me what needs fixin'."

Millie looked at Bud like she was going to burst out laughing. Bud thought Howie might be kidding him, but he also knew Howie didn't have pets, so maybe he wasn't.

"Howie, just tell him we'll do it. The county has been wanting to do that for a long time, and he wouldn't let us. Those dogs are his family and he treats them better than most people treat their kids, but there's a limit to what he can keep up with. He lets them run sometimes, and they're getting to be a problem. I think he's finally coming around."

"10-4, Sheriff."

"Howie, how's the river holding up?"

"It's holding up real good. It just topped the diversion dam. I'm on my way to help the mayor evacuate a couple of farmers who refused to budge. I bet they'll budge now, 'cause it's hard *not* to budge when you're floating. 10-4, over."

Just like Howie, to hold back the best for last, Bud thought, wishing he were down there. But he had serious business at hand.

They pulled into the little juniper grove, and Bud cut the engine. He was pretty certain that Millie knew the right questions to ask and was ready. She had Bud's little voice-activated recorder in her pocket, all ready to go.

Millie walked down the road, in full sight, while Bud snuck down behind the cabin, crouching under a window, hidden by the little lean-to that had held Joe's rock collection.

Now, if the murderer would just keep their date, Bud thought. Bud had told him he would be back this afternoon, but he knew there were no guarantees.

Finally, after awhile, Millie went back outside and yelled, "Anybody here?"

Now he could hear someone coming, the footsteps crunching on the dead scrub-oak leaves.

Millie was back inside the cabin when the person entered, and Bud could hear her let out a gasp. He hadn't wanted to tell her, as she wouldn't believe him, plus he was kind of wanting a final test of her innocence. There was no doubt in his mind now, she'd had nothing to do with the murder.

"I can't believe my eyes," she said and immediately started crying. "I can't believe it."

"What are you doing here, Millie?"

Bud knew that voice. He'd been right all along. Now to get the evidence on tape. Without it, he didn't have much of a case. He hoped Millie wouldn't change her mind. He was too far away to record anything, even if he had another recorder.

Millie said, "I had no idea, I thought..."

"You thought what?"

"Are you a murderer?"

She was getting right to the point. Bud could tell she didn't want to do this.

"Why should I admit anything to you?"

"Because we're friends. I stood by you. Because you care about me and I care about you."

"I killed the guy, Millie, but it was accidental. I feel terrible about it."

"What happened?"

"He was going to rat on me. I shot him, close range, but I was mad. I didn't really think about what I was doing. I was scared."

"Scared? Why?"

"He was going to undo everything I'd worked so hard for. I finally was getting ahead financially, and he was going to tell the feds."

"The feds?"

"Yes, they were investigating everything. They knew what we were doing, and he'd made a plea bargain with them to get off. It meant ratting me out."

"My God. How did you know all that?"

"He told me."

"You didn't have to kill him, did you?"

"I told you, it was an accident. I had just meant to scare him, make him think that I would kill him if he ratted me out. I wanted him to leave. But it ended up killing him. I was so close it went right into his heart."

"How did you make it look like an animal attack?"

"That was also accidental. I heard someone coming, so I dragged his body over into an alcove over there in the cliffs to hide it. I was scared to death, Millie. You know me, I'm not a killer, I'm a caring gentle person. I left it over there, and somehow the coyotes got into it. They really chewed him up. You couldn't even see the gun wounds."

"Then why did you drag him back into the cabin?"

"I wanted him out of the alcove, I had stuff in there, and I didn't want anyone finding it. I was gonna bury him, but I was too late, someone found him while I was gone looking for a shovel."

"What kind of stuff?"

"I had a Bigfoot suit. I was trying to scare people off."

"Where in the world did you get a Bigfoot suit?"

"My cousin over in Salina ordered it for me. He has a small film company, does stuff for the travel councils. It cost a fortune, but like I said, I was making good money—for a change."

"So you stood there in that damn suit and harassed me all night long, scaring the crap outta me? That's pretty low."

"I don't know what you're talking about."

"And you broke into my cafe. Not once, but twice. Some friend. Why did you write a note saying you were sorry?"

"How did you know I wrote that note? I tried to make it look different. I'm sorry, Millie, but I had to have those paintings. They were evidence. And I'm sorry for sneaking around your house, but you had the last one in there. Where is it? I want it back."

"Evidence of what?"

"Look, Millie, you had to have figured it out. Where did you think I was getting money? I was digging up pots and stuff and selling it. Carlos was my middle man. I had no idea where the stuff went. But if someone were to make the connection between an illegal pot and the paintings, I'd be screwed."

"Who's Carlos?"

"The Mexican sheepherder. Say, do you have any idea who stole my rock collection?"

It was all starting to come together.

Millie said, "Look, you need to turn yourself in, it would make it easier for you in the long run, just like Bud told you last night."

"Bud? I never talked to Bud. All I did was whack him on the head. I feel kind of bad about that."

"Not as bad as I felt," Bud said, rounding the corner, gun in hand, standing in the open door.

"Joe, you're under arrest."

Just then, a stiff breeze hit the door, slamming it into Bud and knocking him off balance. It was only for a moment, but it was all Joe needed to push past and run like the wind.

Bud was disappointed. He had no intention of shooting Joe, but now they'd have to get a manhunt going. He himself was way too off-balance to chase Joe anywhere, that's part of why the door had caught him off guard.

"Bud, he's getting away."

"I can't go after him, Millie. Not in my condition, with a concussion." He felt helpless.

"Maybe he'll disappear into the canyons." Millie sounded almost hopeful.

"Thanks for your help, Mill. I hope it's all on tape, but if not, there are two witnesses, and that will hold up in court."

Bud wondered how they could have a trial when the defendant was missing.

Millie handed Bud the recorder.

He said, "Sounds like we got it. Thanks. I know that was hard for you to do."

"The hardest part was seeing who I was talking to. It's not often you get to talk to a dead man. In fact, wasn't there a book or something called *Dead Men Don't Talk?*"

"I dunno, I never read mysteries, myself."

Just then, the sound of a gunshot echoed off the cliffs.

Bud and Millie took off towards the sound, which seemed to be down in Eagle Canyon. They went down the trail and had almost reached the alcove where Millie had been stuck when they heard the sound of an ATV, then another, fading into the distance.

All was quiet.

They stood there for a bit, wondering what was going on, then decided to head on back to the cafe. There wasn't much they could do at this point, and Bud still wasn't feeling too well.

Wherever Joe Swasey was, the odds were good he would never be found, as he knew the canyons of the Swell like no one else on Earth.

38

Bud groaned as they pulled up to the cafe. Now there were two black Land Rovers there, the stretch limo and a regular one. He decided the latter probably belonged to Doc Richardson.

When she left with Bud, Millie had left the cafe unlocked with a "Be Back Soon" sign on the door. A couple of bikers were sitting at the bar, drinking coffee, which they'd poured themselves. They were about to make some sandwiches when Millie went over and took their order.

Sure enough, the TV people were in the back booth. They were talking to the doctor. A woman motioned for Bud not to talk.

"I still think Gigantopithecus could very well be the ancestor of Bigfoot," one said. "Anyway, since you're a medical doctor, has anyone around these parts ever come into your office with wounds you could attribute to probably being from a Bigfoot?"

"Oh, more often than you might think," answered Doc.

Bud realized they were interviewing him on camera. He sat down quietly and listened.

"Would you care to elaborate on that?"

"Why, just a short time ago there was a fellow killed up here on the Swell by a Bigfoot. I'm the county coroner, I don't know if you knew that. I cover two counties, and I had the privilege of doing the coroner's report."

It suddenly occurred to Bud that he had never read the report on what was supposedly Joe's body. So much for being thorough. But Doc probably hadn't even done much of one, given the state of things.

Doc continued. "Believe me, you don't want to go there, so don't ask what it looks like to be killed by a Bigfoot. But he wasn't the first, by any means. I've seen occasional Bigfoot kill for years, but we always just say it's an animal kill in the report, you know, lions and such."

"You have lions out here?"

"Of course, lots of them, especially up here on the Swell. They come around the cafe all the time wanting handouts, and people have even witnessed them cooperating in Bigfoot hunts. Lions and Bigfoots. The Bigfoot would flush out the game and the lions would chase it down. Deer and such."

"You mean mountain lions, not real lions."

"That's it, cougars," Doc answered.

Millie sat down next to Bud and snickered, "What a con artist."

The interviewer continued. "Have you ever seen a Bigfoot, Doctor?"

"No, I haven't personally seen one, but I have many friends who have. One of them is sitting right over there." With that, he pointed directly at Bud.

Just then, the cafe door opened and in came a tall man dressed somewhat like a local, but who Bud immediately knew wasn't because of something he couldn't quite put his finger on. He was walking too stiff or something, thought Bud. Then he saw the sneakers and knew that was the difference. Everyone in these parts wore boots.

Roger immediately came in behind him, which surprised Bud.

They came over to Bud.

"Let me introduce myself. I'm Jack Nelson, Investigator with the National Park Service," said the man.

Bud stood and shook his hand.

"Nice to meet you." Bud then turned to Roger and said, "What are you doing here? I thought you went home."

"I got a bit sidetracked. These guys have been looking for Joe Swasey and thought he was dead, but it seems not. I wasn't aware that was the name of the guy they were looking for, lame as that sounds."

Roger continued, "After you told me what you were going to do later this afternoon, go arrest him, I called Jack. He works with my wife—well, did before she took some time off and we got pregnant. He's been on this case for months. He's the one who was about to arrest Joe when he disappeared. They never were really sure where to look for him, as the Mexican sheepherder was their go between."

"Arrest him for what?"

"Stealing pots, grave digging, and selling antiquities on the black market. One of the places Joe had been was down in Horseshoe Canyon, which is part of Canyonlands National Park. They've already arrested the three men on the other end of the pipeline, but couldn't find Joe. They actually quit looking, as they thought he was dead. And they thought Carlos Gonzales had somehow slipped back into Mexico. So see, Bud, I didn't really abandon you. It just took longer than I thought for these guys to get here."

"But now, Sheriff," Jack Nelson said. "We need your assistance. We have Swasey handcuffed outside, my partner is out there, and we'd like you to lock him up."

Bud answered, "I'm sorry, but I don't have a jail."

The man looked surprised.

Bud added, "You'll have to take him to Castle Dale. That's where the courthouse is."

Bud didn't want to go outside and see Joe, as he knew he'd be seeing plenty of him soon enough in court. Maybe he'd buy some of Joe's art someday, as he would have plenty of time in prison to paint.

Bud continued, "And now please excuse me. Now that I've seen how it's properly done, I have a film interview to tend to."

∽

Soon, Roger and Bud were coming down off the Swell in the old red Bronco. Roger was going to spend the night at Bud's, then Bud would get him home the next day on the train. Hopefully Roger's wife would wait to have the baby.

Bud asked, "Rog, if you knew about the feds working on the pot-looting case and looking for Joe, why didn't you tell me?"

Roger answered, "I didn't know it was Joe. My wife told me about it, and I honestly thought it was down around Blanding somewhere, as there had been some stuff going on down there at Cedar Mesa. I wasn't really paying attention. She does that, she comes and talks to me while I'm trying to study. Maybe it's because I'm always trying to study. But hey, that's over now. I'm now a real geologist!"

"Congrats," Bud said. "It's a big achievement."

"Thanks. I've never worked so hard in my life. But Bud, how did you figure out it wasn't Joe's body?"

Bud drew in his breath. "Well, it took awhile, as you know. I had a weird dream, and it was telling me that Joe hadn't been killed, but I got all sidetracked, thinking Doc Richardson had killed him. Prof Krider warned me, he said to look for the one who had the most to lose, and I figured it was the doc. But in reality, it was Joe, as he'd just figured out what it meant to have money."

He continued. "But I think my subconscious had picked up on a number of clues and that's why the dream. First, the photos of the body—it took me a long time, but I finally figured out the guy was too small to be Joe. But there were other clues, too."

"First, he was wearing expensive boots from Mexico. That's something a non-Mexican around here wouldn't be into, it's cultural. The Mexican guys are big on nice clothing, but even after he came into money, Joe wouldn't have worn those kind of boots. And second, the silver cross—Catholics carry crosses a lot, and many Mexicans are Catholic. I knew Joe wasn't, his family had been Mormons, the ones who were religious, that is, and Mormons don't wear crosses. But third, the ashes test was the final clue—cyanide—a moderate but not lethal dose."

"What did that show?"

"That the guy was a sheepherder, and I knew he had to be older. Sheep dip, the stuff they dipped the sheep in for tick control, used to have cyanide in it, and a lot of these older guys are carrying it around in their bodies, though it hasn't killed them, not yet, anyway. A lot of the old sheep dip places are toxic waste sites."

"And then fourth, I got an email from a family in Mexico looking for their dad. A sheepherder. I'm going to send them the silver cross Todd found."

Bud paused, pushing his sunglasses back up, then continued.

"But another possible clue was the hamburger. Someone had recently been eating a hamburger, as it was fresh. Joe ate a lot of hamburgers, maybe even some he'd rustled himself, according to Henry Tidwell. But I sent that hamburger in for a test, and as soon as I can get some of Joe's DNA, it will add to the proof that he was there in the cabin after the guy had been murdered, not that we need that proof any more. I'm still trying to figure out where he got it, as Millie said he hadn't come into the cafe."

Roger was silent for a minute.

"Bud," he said. "Todd told me that was his hamburger. He'd been in shock and forgot all about it when you asked him. He wanted me to tell you that, and I forgot."

Bud started laughing. "Well I'll be darned. You win some, you lose some. But that hamburger was the only thing that gave me the courage to get Millie in there to record his confession. Without it, I wouldn't have figured I had a case and would have probably let it go. Thank Todd for me, will you?"

He paused as they came to Spotted Wolf Canyon.

"Oh, and next time you see him, ask Professor Cole if his attorney ever got back with him about that non-confidentiality agreement. I hope those guys found whatever they were looking for. My guess was uranium."

"Your guess would be right," Roger replied. "Professor Cole took those samples I found at the cabin, by the way, and they're really hot, as in radioactive hot. That's why he and Jimmy Wilson had been up at

Swasey's cabin, they'd heard he had some hot rocks. I overheard them talking about it just a little bit ago. Prof's going back up there with a bunch from Mancos Resources in a couple of weeks. They're all fired up about a possible strike. Too bad they can't ask Joe where he got them."

"Maybe we can work out some kind of plea bargain with that in it," Bud laughed.

Roger replied, "Problem is, it's against the law for them to talk about it, even if Joe would talk."

They laughed, then dropped down off the Swell and saw the lights of Green River in the distance.

39

It was late morning, and Wilma Jean and Roger were sitting on the bungalow's big back porch, drinking coffee, laughing and having a great time. Hoppie and Pierre were hanging out with them, Pierre in Roger's lap.

Bud was glad Rog liked Wilma Jean. He was hoping he'd stay in touch with them and bring his new family down to visit.

Bud went into the living room and sat down in his big leather recliner. He dialed Prof Krider.

"Prof, I solved the case. Do I still have a job? 'Cause I'm going to resign today, if I do."

"Bud, of course. We're flooding out, and I could use you right now."

"Is it too early to talk about salary?"

"No, that's just good business. We both have to know where we stand. Let me know what you're making and I'll add 5k to it. I think I have a good idea already, since it's public record, and I saw it in the paper awhile ago. And insurance, of course. We'll make it fair, whatever we have to do. Can you come out now?"

"No, I'm technically still sheriff. But I'll let you know after I talk to the mayor."

"Bud, can I ask who killed Joe, or is it improper at this point?"

"No, it's OK. Nobody killed Joe, he's still alive. I'll stop by later and explain it all."

"Sounds like maybe the plot for my next book," Krider answered.

Bud now dialed the mayor's office.

"Rich, it's Bud, how's it going?"

"OK, Bud. Glad you're back in town and congrats on the arrest. That sounds like a tough case, but you broke it wide open."

Bud decided the mayor must have been talking to Howie, who had obviously listened in when Bud called the jail in Castle Dale from the office yesterday evening to let them know the feds were bringing in Joe.

"It was tough, Mayor, but not as tough as what I'm about to do. I'd like to come in and talk with you."

"Sure, sure. But if it's about a raise, you know as well as I that we're sinking. Just like those melon farms out by the river."

"Yeah, and I need to get back on that. But no, Mayor, this is kind of the opposite of asking for a raise. You're going to have a bit more money, 'cause your sheriff is leaving. I wanted to tell you in person, Rich."

"I think I'm about to have a real bad day, Bud, but come on down. I'll be thinking of ways to talk you out of it in the meantime."

"OK, and I want to reclaim my old Bronco. You guys have the money for a new vehicle, so I want to cancel your lease. I have to take a friend to the train station first, then I'll be over."

"Not a problem, Bud. I'll be here."

Bud and Wilma Jean stood at the train station, waiting to put Roger on the Amtrak for Salt Lake City. He was excited.

"I've never ridden a train before. I feel like a little kid."

"It will take you a few hours to get home, so enjoy it. Somebody will pick you up there, right?"

"My brother. Say, Sheriff, am I still a deputy?"

"You are," Bud said. "But for only about another hour. Say, be prepared to ride the train back down here after the baby's born to come get your pay."

"What? How does that work?" Roger asked.

"Well, you might not want to bring the baby, though we'd love to see it and meet its mom. It might be a bit too rough of a ride back for them at this point, and it always sticks a bit in reverse."

"What on God's green Earth are you talking about, Bud?" Wilma Jean asked, shaking her head. "Is that head injury still bothering you?" She laughed.

"This," he replied, holding up the keys to his old Bronco. "From now on, I'm going to be driving Krider's new Ford pickup around. And saving up for a Toyota FJ."

Wilma Jean's eyebrows went up. "Did you take the job for sure, hon?"

"I just talked to Krider. I'm going down to resign right after this."

"They'll miss you, Sheriff," Roger said. "And so will I. What you're doing means a lot to me. I'll be back soon."

With that, he stepped up into the coach and was gone.

40

Bud sat in his office, his feet up on the desk, kicked back in the big easy chair. He'd already put all his office stuff out in the Bronco, taken off the light bar, and brought the siren in. He would go down to the highway department shop tomorrow to have the radio removed by their radio technician.

He watched the kids across the street at Howie's, thinking this would be the last time he sat in this chair and watched them throw water at each other.

He felt a bit nostalgic. He would start at the farm technically day after tomorrow, but he knew as soon as he finished up here he'd be out there.

The flood waters were receding, and there would be a big mess to clean up. He wanted to be there to make sure it was done right. Krider had already hired two workers to help him with that and then the reseeding afterwards.

His cell phone rang. It was Wilma Jean.

"Hon, you're gonna be here for dinner tonight, aren't you? And that's not a question like it sounds, but an order. We're having company. Somebody you won't want to miss."

"Who?"

"Doc Richardson and Millie Mortenson are stopping by on their way through. They really want to see you. Me, too, I really want to see you. I'm making fried chicken and mashed potatoes, gravy, rolls, and salad."

"Hon, I wouldn't miss it for anything. I'm almost done here, then I'm stopping by the farm for an hour, then I'll be home."

"Perfect," she said. "Oh, I almost forgot. Larry called, and he's in town, and I invited him, too. You guys can all talk about the good old days. OK, see you later."

Just then, Howie came into the office. He was upset.

"What's wrong, Deputy?"

"I don't know what's going to happen over there at Howie's."

"How so, Howie?"

"I did an owner carry on it, and the guy is now three payments behind. It's no wonder, letting a bunch of kids run it. I had built that up into a good restaurant, and it's getting ruined."

"You may end up with it back."

"I know, and I may have to go run it again."

"But Howie, how can you do that and be sheriff, too?"

Howie gave Bud a look. How did Bud know he was after his job?

"Whattya mean, Sheriff? Me, sheriff?"

"I just resigned, Deputy. The mayor said I could offer you the job on his behalf. I gave two weeks notice, but I have two weeks' vacation coming, and if you take the job, I can leave right now. If you're interested, he wants you to call him. It would be an interim position until the term ends and they elect someone, but they would probably end up electing you, if you did a good job. You'd get a bit of a raise. Are you interested?"

Howie looked shocked. He'd be a fool not to take it. His ex-wife over in Castle Dale would have to eat crow after telling him he would never amount to anything.

"I think I'm very interested," he replied. "Starting when?"

"Right now. I'm almost out the door, Sheriff."

"You're really not the sheriff anymore?"

"Nope, not if you take it."

"I could arrest you?"

"Only if I broke the law."

"Just kidding."

"You have to be careful to not let the power go to your head, Sheriff."

"Yes, I could see that," Howie answered thoughtfully. "I do want the job, Bud. I really do."

"It might mean some long hours."

"I'm used to that, running a cafe."

"Well, then, call the mayor."

Bud sat and listened as Howie called the mayor, accepting the position of Interim Sheriff. Bud then congratulated him when he hung up the phone.

Howie grinned. "I guess I'm now officially the Sheriff of Emery County."

"Yup," Bud answered. "Here's my badge—it's yours now. I think you set some kind of record for quickest deputy to make sheriff. Don't forget about that new vehicle. Did the mayor tell you they're still thinking of relocating the office to Castle Dale when the next term starts?"

Howie groaned. "Castle Dale? I hate that town. That's where my ex lives."

"I know," Bud said. "But at least you have time to reconsider it. You're just the Interim Sheriff. You can go back to the cafe when election time comes if you decide not to move."

Howie relaxed. "You're right. I may have to."

Just then the phone rang.

"Sheriff's Office, Sheriff Howie." Howie listened for a bit, then turned to Bud, putting his hand over the receiver.

"Sheriff, it's the Ghost Rock Cafe."

"Sheriff, I'm not the sheriff anymore."

"Dang it, Bud, they want me to come up there. It's almost four o'clock. I won't even get there till dinner time."

"What's the problem?"

"Somebody says a Bigfoot's been trying to break in."

"Tell them you'll be up first thing in the morning."

Howie repeated Bud's advice. He listened for a bit, then said, "I'll be right up," and hung up.

"It's Mr. Samuelson, and he says if I don't come now he'll have my job."

"Howie, maybe he should have your job. He'd learn some respect for us normal people. Besides, they like drama, let them have drama. They can film it."

"You're right, Bud. I'm gonna close up shop and go to Howie's for dinner. To heck with this job. I'll do what I can and then when they elect someone else, I'll run Howie's again. I actually loved that little place and regretted selling it."

"Way to go, Sheriff," Bud high-fived him.

"Thanks, Bud." Howie said, high-fiving him back.

They both walked out the door and on to better things.

ABOUT THE AUTHOR

Chinle Miller writes from southeastern Utah and western Colorado, where she spends most of her time wandering with her dogs. She has an A.S. in Geology, a B.A. in Anthropology and an M.A. in Linguistics.

If you enjoyed this book, you'll also enjoy the other books in the Bud Shumway mystery series:

The Slickrock Cafe
The Paradox Cafe
The No Delay Cafe
The Silver Spur Cafe
The Ice House Cafe
The Rattlesnake Cafe
The Beartooth Cafe
The Melon Rind Cafe
The Cessna Cafe
The Klondike Cafe
The Yellow Cat Cafe
The Swiftcurrent Cafe
The Sunnyside Cafe
The Temple Mountain Cafe

And don't miss *Desert Rats: Adventures in the American Outback, Uranium Daughter, Wandering off the Map,* and *The Impossibility of Loneliness,* also by Chinle Miller.

And if you enjoy Bigfoot stories, you'll love *Rusty Wilson's Bigfoot Campfire Stories* and his many other Bigfoot books, as well as his popular *Chasing After Bigfoot: My Search for North America's Most Elusive Creature.*

Other offerings from Yellow Cat Publishing include an RV series by RV expert Sunny Skye, which includes *Living the Simple RV Life, The Truth about the RV Life,* and *RVing with Pets,* as well as *Tales of a Campground Host.* And don't forget to check out the books by Sunny's friend, Bob Davidson: *On the Road with Joe* and *Any Road, USA.* And finally, you'll love Roger Dean Miller's comedy thriller, *Bombing Hoffman.*

www.ingramcontent.com/pod-product-compliance
Lightning Source LLC
Chambersburg PA
CBHW051654260626
47170CB00004B/1498